Greenwoman

A Literary Garden of . . .

Fiction ❋ Nonfiction ❋ Poetry ❋ Commentary

Biography ❋ Art ❋ Comics

Volume 2 - George W. Carver

Editor-In-Chief: Sandra Knauf
Second-In-Command: Zora Knauf
Copy Editor and Brilliant-Advisor-
on-Everything-Else: Cheri Colburn

Chief Designer: Sandra Knauf
Art Director: Rachael Davis
Web Designer/Tech. Support: Paul Spielman

Advertising contact: Sandra Knauf
(719) 473-9237
sandra@greenwomanmagazine.com

Greenwoman Magazine
P. O. Box 6587, Colo. Spgs., CO
80934-6587

Attn. retailers: For more information about
selling this marvelous magazine in your store
call 719-473-9237 or write
sandra@greenwomanmagazine.com

ISBN-10: 098970565X
ISBN-13: 978-0-9897056-5-3

www.greenwomanmagazine.com
www.florasforum.com
www.zeraandthegreenman.com
www.greenwomanpublishing.com

Contents

Front cover art by Sandra Knauf featuring Dante Gabriel Rossetti's *Venus Verticordia* (1864-68).

We love Dave Gardner, creator and director of *GrowthBusters.*

Editor's Letter

In Issue #1, I wrote about the transformative power of nature, specifically through gardening, and how *Greenwoman* would explore and celebrate this power through literature and art. Now I have to recognize a more expansive goal. *Greenwoman*'s larger mission is this: To make the world a better place. (There, I wrote it. I admit it.)

Through the years, when I've shared this changing-the-world-through-art idea, I've been called an idealist (can't argue there), a Pollyanna, and even a Don Quixote. Guess what? I don't care one whit. I know art is powerful. It can change the world. My job? To provide the medium. If *Greenwoman*'s mission is naïve, I say a world with more naiveté will surely be a better one.

I was moved to acknowledge this grander notion when Seth Godin's book *Tribes* showed up in my life. I learned about this paradigm-changing book while reading a blog post by Leslie Martin, creator of the sublime natural home and beauty blog "Crunchy Betty." (See page 18 for Leslie's new column.) In that post, Leslie explained her meaning of the word *crunchy*. (*Crunchy* is about striving for a healthy, mindful, beautiful life.) Reading her post, I learned about tribes, both the book and the concept. I also learned that *crunchy* is a tribe!—and that *Greenwoman* is crunchy!

I bought a copy of Godin's book and was reminded that we all seek tribes (groups, clubs, affiliations) that are reflections of ourselves and what we value most. Pondering this, I recognized that *Greenwoman* is a newborn tribe in and of itself; it is also a member of several bigger tribes: author tribes, artist tribes, environmentalist tribes, and so on.

Members of the *Greenwoman* tribe surely love a creative life—one filled with art, writing, and learning. We share a deep love and respect for nature and gardening, and we share a strong sense of responsibility that we are the ones who must help heal our planet. Our serious quest for a better life is enriched by an outrageous sense of humor and a never-ending delight in fun.

My work is to grow this splendid tribe by getting the word out: The *Greenwoman* Tribe is here.

Sharing is another ethic of our tribe, and this issue is an excellent example. Come share in the bounty! I'm especially proud of Cheri Coburn's beautifully-wrought biography of the legendary American scientist, environmentalist, and (quiet) social activist, Dr. George Washington Carver. "GWC" (as we grew to call him in our many emails) is more than an historical figure; he is a man for today—a creator of brilliant solutions for hard times, a champion of lifelong learning, beauty, common sense, and making do with what one has. You'll also love Molly O'Neill's "Rare Breed," about a man who is saving heritage turkey breeds; Michael Stusser's "The Garden Club," a story bursting with humor and heart; and Alissa Johnson's "Naked Tomatoes," a delicately told tale of the changing landscape of love.

Sandra

Sandra Knauf
Editor and Publisher

Zora Knauf,
Editorial Assistant
Extraordinaire

Contributors

 **Cheri Colburn** (who wrote "George Washington Carver: Grandfather of Sustainability") is a writer, editor, and gardener who lives, works, and raises human beings in Colorado Springs, Colorado. Her "likes" include hiking, the sound of her children's voices, and long days digging in the dirt. Her "dislikes" include dieting, deadlines, and quitting bad habits.

 **Rachael Davis** is a fine artist currently pursuing a MFA in Fort Collins, Colorado. Rachael says she's delighted to have the opportunity to collaborate on *Greenwoman Magazine* as it keeps her connected with the pulse of the community and in sync with her lifelong environmental focus. Her sensibility towards stewardship of the earth manifests in gardening, activism, art making and, most importantly, being a whole mother and human being.

 Artist and college student **Karley Ford** has been making art since she was "a wee one." She's currently studying graphic design, a huge passion she hopes to utilize in the future. She loves painting as well and has six years of hands-in-the-dirt horticultural experience working at her grandparents' nursery and landscaping business, Stone Path Gardens in Colorado Springs, Colorado.

 **Kim Gravestock**'s garden design work (she owns From the Ground Up) can be seen at The Cliffhouse, a five-star hotel in Manitou Springs, Colorado. Over the last 15 years, she's been a beekeeper, a Beekeeping School Coordinator, and Vice President for the Pikes Peak Beekeeping Association. She has also been a featured speaker at the Pikes Peak Landscape Symposium and an instructor for the CSU Master Gardener program. Photographing plants, bugs, and other wonders of Nature is her latest endeavor.

 Among poet **Lois Beebe Hayna's** accomplishments are a Fellowship in Poetry by the state of Colorado, a Doctor of Letters Honorary Degree from Regis University, and a Golden Quill award. Regis University named a creative writing center for Hayna in 2009. Her books of poetry include: *Casting Two Shadows*, *Keeping Still*, *Behind the Mirror*, *Northern Gothic*, *Never Trust a Crow* and B*ook of Charms*. She has also spoken eloquently on conservation: www. coloradoconservationtrust.org/uncategorized/97-year-old-lois-hayna-on-land-conservation/

 **Robin Intemann** (who interviewed Christa DeCiccio and contributed a book review for this issue) includes among her passions food, books, friends, and family (although not necessarily in that order). The one thing she enjoys about winter gardening is not having to weed. Robin teaches journalism, and has contributed freelance work to numerous area publications. She recently started a blog on books and food: www.bluepagespecial.com.

 **Alissa Johnson** (author of "Naked Tomatoes") moved from the cities of Minnesota to the mountains of Colorado where she is learning to relate to a land governed by snow and thin air. Follow her journey at www.alissajohnson.wordpress.com

Contributors

Pat Kennelly (who wrote a book review for this issue) is a freelance writer, poet, and gardener who lives and works in Colorado Springs, Colorado. Most recently her work has appeared in *The Denver Post*, *Haibun Today*, *Articus,* and *Messages from the Hidden Lake*.

Elisabeth Kinsey (who pens the column "Sex in the Garden") teaches writing online, lives in New York, pines away for Half Moon Bay and publishes in *The Denver Post* and various journals. Her hands are imminently dirty. She may or may not be related to the late Dr. Alfred Kinsey.

Dianne Kornberg's photography and photo-based work has been exhibited nationally and internationally for more than two decades. She is represented in numerous museum, public and private collections; her work is the subject of two monographs, and is included in several anthologies. She is a Professor Emerita at Pacific Northwest College of Art in Portland, Oregon, and has her studio in the San Juan Islands in Washington State.

Kathleen Lindemann (who has a book review and art featured in this issue) is currently a Journalism Major and a tutor at Pikes Peak community College. She loves naure and writing. "Her experiences make her the unulitmate free-spirited woman," says classmate Kristopher Poskey. "Her life depicts the story of many Americans after the post-1960s great depression, a life full of adventure." She earned her degree in Environmental Technology in 1997. Her new passion is to lead people to the better future of green living, through research and writing.

Leslie Martin (who writes the column "Crunchy Betty") is a full-time blogger and freelance writer from Manitou Springs, CO. She regularly puts food on her face for her blog, *Crunchy Betty*, and has published one book—*Crunchy Betty's Food on Your Face for Acne and Oily Skin*—but remains furiously typing away at her next three. After a brief stint as a professional model, Leslie now champions the idea that beauty is in everything and everyone, and that conscious living is the only way to a peaceful, happier future.

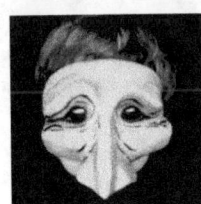

Poet **Carolyn Moore**'s three chapbooks won their respective competitions, as has her book-length collection, *Instructions for Traveling Light*, pending publication as winner of the Deep Bowl Press Poetry Prize. She taught at Humboldt State University (Arcata, California) until able to eke out a living as a freelance writer and researcher. She now lives on the last vestige of the family farm, where she installed an 8' deer fence to protect her flower and vegetable gardens but still shares the 25-tree orchard with the cloven-hoofed marauders.

Dan Murphy (who writes the column "Slow Ride") is a seasoned zine writer (*The Juniper*, *Elephant Mess*) and proponent of the slow life. His long-time passions include bike riding, skateboarding, punk rock, and gardening. His new interests include botany, ecology, wildflowers, and lichens. Dan has a B.S. in horticulture and is pursuing an M.S. in biology involving a thesis on green roof technology research. www.juniperbug.blogspot.com

Contributors

Molly O'Neill is the former food columnist for *The New York Times Magazine* and was the host of the PBS series *Great Food*. Her work has appeared in many national magazines. She is the author of a memoir, *Mostly True*, and four cookbooks: *One Big Table: A Portrait of American Cooking, A Well-Seasoned Appetite, The Pleasure of Your Company*, and the award-winning *New York Cookbook*. She divides her time between New York City and upstate New York.

At age 20, **Cynthia Rosi** (who wrote "Tuscan Roots") emigrated from Seattle to London, determined to write for a living and to marry the Anglo-Italian boy she'd met at a bus-stop during a University exchange program. They spent many happy summers in Tuscany, and Cynthia loved apprenticing in her husband's aunt's kitchen. Her daughter has followed in those footsteps, and learned last summer how to make homemade ravioli. Aunty Mabu inspired Cynthia's garden, her flock of chickens, and her best meals. Cynthia blogs at www.simplyhugyourself.com

DB Rudin (who writes the column "Creature Feature") is an environmental education consultant, elementary school teacher, and the Education Coordinator at Venetucci Farm, an 190-acre historic farm in Colorado Springs, Colorado. He offers programs through Colorado Critter Encounters, which includes hands-on programs for kids on nature and conservation, and a class for those who tend the soil, The Good, the Bad and the Beautiful: Bugs 101 for Gardeners. www.cocritterencounters.com

Larry Stebbins (who wrote the "Growing Locally" column in this issue and a book review) is the founder and director of Pikes Peak Urban Gardens, a botanist, retired science teacher and has over 40 years experience as a biodynamic and organic gardener.

J.D. Smith (third from left) has received a Fellowship in Poetry from the United States National Endowment for the Arts, and his third collection, *Labor Day at Venice Beach*, is forthcoming in 2012. Smith's first essay collection, *Dowsing and Science*, was recently published by *Texas Review Press*, listed in *The Huffington Post* as one of the United States' "fifteen feisty indepedent publishers." He provides periodic updates at www.jdsmithwriter.blogspot.com

Michael A. Stusser (who wrote "Garden Club") is a Seattle-based freelance writer and game inventor. His first book, *The Dead Guy Interviews: Conversations with 45 of the Most Accomplished, Notorious, and Deceased Personalities in History* (Penguin Publishing) was released to critical acclaim in 2008. Stusser is a columnist for mental_floss magazine and his work is frequently published by *Yoga International*, *Seattle Weekly*, and the *New York Times Syndicate*.

Eva Syrovy (who wrote the essay for this issue's "Top Dressing") is an immigrant from the Czech Republic who has been a daughter and mother (two boys, one grown), an oil field "frack rat" and teacher, a diligent runner and cyclist, a lazy gardener, a decent cook and quilter, and a lousy housekeeper. Her writing, about the kids she mothers and teaches, history, and the environment, has been most regularly published in the *Colorado Springs Business Journal* and *The Denver Post*.

Contributors

Benjamin Vogt (who wrote "*Pulsatilla Vulgaris*—Pasque Flower") is the author of the poetry collections *Afterimage* (SFA Press) and *Without Such Absence* (Finishing Line Press). He has a Ph.D. from the University of Nebraska-Lincoln. Benjamin's nonfiction and poetry have been nominated for a Pushcart Prize, and have appeared in over fifty journals, newspapers, anthologies, and textbooks, including *American Life in Poetry*, *Crab Orchard Review*, *Orion*, and *The Sun*. He lives in Lincoln, Nebraska with his wife, where he owns a native plant garden consulting business, Monarch Gardens.

Seattle native **Carolyne Wright** has published nine books of poetry, four collections of poetry in translation from Spanish and Bengali and a volume of essays. Her most recent collections are *Mania Klepto: the Book of Eulene*; *A Change of Maps*; and *Seasons of Mangoes and Brainfire*, winner of the Blue Lynx Prize and American Book Award. A poem of hers appears in *The Best American Poetry 2009*, and in *The Pushcart Prize XXXIV: Best of the Small Presses* (2010). She teaches for the Northwest Institute of Literary Arts' Whidbey Writers Workshop MFA program.

Notes (on our first issue)

I've been fascinated with seed storage and procurement for a while now, [and] there is a great article on that very subject in here that I really dug. I also really enjoyed the articles entitled 'Organicize Me' where a dude goes one month eating and drinking nothing but organic products (prices included), and a personal account of life in the medicinal medical marijuana world ('Hello, Doobie Tuesday') that helped this confusingly great idea come to life for me. This is a excellent first issue with a hell of a lot of soul that today, is more important than ever. Order it, read it, live it.
—Randy Spaghetti

To be honest, I wasn't sure I really wanted fiction in a gardening magazine...but my favorite part in this first issue is the short story *A Human Birth* by Bruce Holland Rogers. I know something is good when I can't stop thinking about it, when I want to tell all my gardening friends to read it, so here I am saying "read it."
—Diana Capen

I think this magazine will be one of the best gifts 2011 has given humanity and I'm absolutely serious about this. I hope you will check it out. When I did that, I clicked immediately on the subscription button and signed myself up. Now for those of you who know me, you will know this is significant because I have a very strict rule about not purchasing anything over the internet. This was one of my very very few exceptions to that rule, in fact, I think it may be the only exception I've made to date in this regards.
—Tammi Hartung

Why is it now rare for people to express passion, unconditional kindness, basic appreciation for the little blessings of life? Apparently, I'm not the only one who feels like this and am thrilled to see the birth of a magazine like *Greenwoman Magazine*. . . Could this be a sign that there are enough of us left to want to reinvent the world with new OLD values? A world with heart? A world where technology and profit can exist but aren't EVERYTHING? . . . I have great hopes for this little magazine. Perhaps it will reinstate the success of magazines. Of quality. Of responsible caring. If there are enough of us, we can make this a better world. One magazine, one article, one plant, one poem, one picture—one person at a time. Are you a part of the revolution? This might even be fun!
—Jane Gates Schwartz

Creating Simplicity

Ever since I was a teenager I have had an interest in and affection for local music. Perhaps it is because I came of age in a small, rural town where my only opportunities to see big bands were either at the state fair (where the old, washed-up acts often perform) or by driving four hours across state lines. The latter was not an option I had the means to regularly exploit, so whenever word spread about local shows, I made it a point to be there. Combine the circumstances of my youth with my long-time interest in independent and underground music, and you will start to see the profound connection I have to small venues, local bands, lo-fi, and minimalism. You don't need a huge stage and a 7-minute long guitar solo to play rock music—a bunch of sweaty kids at a house show can attest to that.

by
Dan Murphy

Have you ever experienced music without electricity? It was in the living room of a stranger's house in Boise, Idaho where I learned that the simplest set up could be the most beautiful and most rewarding. Jason Anderson was singing his heart out to a small group of punks all cuddled up on couches or lounging on the floor; and then there was me, propped up against the wall bobbing my head. All except for the lighting, the show was completely unplugged. It didn't matter that I didn't know anybody there—it was an environment that was comfortable, communal, and friendly. It was more than just the passionate lyrics and heartfelt choruses that drew me in: it was the freedom from convention and the defiant rejection of what it means to put on a rock show. That night I learned that if we want to experience something genuine and momentous, we are going to have to create it ourselves. Not only that, but things don't have to be grandiose to be memorable. I rode my bike home that night feeling empowered and free, spreading my arms out like wings as though I could fly.

Do we need all the stuff we have? I oftentimes wonder if we are fooling ourselves. We work and toil our lives away to pay for things that are far beyond necessity. An education is a good thing. A comfortable place to live and food on the table, we need this. Consistent contact with good friends and family, that is what sustains us. A healthy body and mind and a clean and safe environment, these are good things. But the rest? The rest is probably just excess. Do you need more cowbell in your epic, rock 'n' roll jam? Probably not. Must you have the laser light show and all the smoke machines to prove to the world what a guitar god you are? I don't think so. If we can learn to dance without it, we're probably fine.

That is the beauty of simple living. As we endeavor to live smaller and more mindful lives, we will begin to see how we can pare things down, cut things out, and get by without it. We can learn to find enjoyment in the moment and purpose in the process. We will realize that we don't need to travel across the country to find entertainment or spend half of our life savings to have a good time. Beauty surrounds us, and opportunity abounds.

However, these things may not seem so obvious at first. Answers may not just come to us by accident. Instead, we must go searching for them. We may have to find the courage to begin to build before we realize what it is we are building. Over time we will develop a taste and a love for simpler things, especially as we debunk the myths that encourage us to seek out extravagance and excess. If the things we love and need the most don't exist in our immediate vicinity, we will need to create them. We must become the creators of the worlds we'd like to see and inhabit—and we must do it ourselves, because if we don't, we may not like the outcome, and if we wait for someone else to do it, it may not happen.

I not only enjoy hearing music, I enjoy creating it. I am not a great guitar player by any means. Sure, I can strum a few chords and pick a few notes, but if you were to ask me to hammer out one of the classics, I would reluctantly shrug my shoulders and shake my head. "Sorry, man," I would likely say, "I don't know that one." I mostly make up my own songs. I play the same few chords over and over, and I improvise as I go. I don't have a band backing me up; instead it's just me in my apartment bedroom, rocking out. I have no clue what it must sound like to anyone who catches an earful, and I realize that I will never compare to any of the guitar greats.

All I know is that when my amplifier is cranked and I am in the zone, it feels spectacular! It's not because I'm making great music, it's because I'm creating something real. It's simply a moment that I have made. It's small, but it has the potential to be powerful and transcendent. It may not be perfect, but it's all I really need. ✺

Naked
Tomatoes
by
Alissa Johnson

Illustration by Rachael Davis

Glass jars of home-canned tomatoes fill the cupboard over my refrigerator, '50s icons in a 21st century kitchen. If I could, I would pull one down, unscrew the gold metal band and pop off the lid underneath to release the fresh aroma of tomato. It would be a reminder of summer's abundance, a buoy against the ice and snow covering the ground and the downward slide of the thermometer. But I have moved out of the house while my husband and I sort our belongings, and I saw no room in transient living for fragile, glass jars.

I almost skipped canning this year. The end of tomato season appeared unhurried on the horizon when tomatoes first arrived at the farmer's market in July. And then I was lying in bed on an October Saturday, ticking off fall chores: change the storm windows, put the garden to bed, give the compost one final turn. I turned to Chris.

"We won't miss canned tomatoes, will we?"

"It'll be worth it in January," he said. "I'll work in the garden while you can the tomatoes. We'll do the windows tomorrow."

We drove to the farmers' market and wandered up and down rows of stalls in the YWCA parking lot. Bushels of canning tomatoes sat on the ground at every stand, their skins pocked by small scars and bruises. But their scent was fresh, and the autumn air sharp and brisk. The growing length of the sun's shadows enticed us to grab as much produce as we could. At home, vegetables flowed across the kitchen and spilled onto the floor: peppers for roasting, Roma tomatoes for drying, winter squash stacked in a corner and the canning tomatoes waiting on the floor.

The enamel canning pot dwarfed the stove and the smaller pot of boiling water beside it. I dropped several tomatoes into the smaller pot and watched as bubbles rose up out of their scars. Fishing them out with a slotted spoon, I slipped them into a bowl of ice water, shocking the tomatoes so that a gentle squeeze slid their deep red flesh out from under their skins. Juice ran down my fingers and dripped on the counter, and the pile of naked tomatoes grew.

I started canning the year Chris and I moved into our first apartment. At the time I worked each summer as a camp director, four hours north in Ely, Minnesota. On days off, I borrowed the neighbor's chocolate Lab and hiked through red and white pines over glacier-carved bedrock. I picked wild berries as we went: June strawberries in the sandy soils along the road, July raspberries in a sunny patch where trees had collapsed during a storm, and August blueberries nestled among lichen on top of a rocky hill overlooking the lake. While I filled my buckets, the dog ate blueberries right off the bush. I returned to our two-room cabin with too many berries to eat. Before long the freezer was full, and it became clear the berries would never survive the drive back to the Cities in September. I borrowed canning equipment from my neighbor and learned to make jam. The cabin windows grew dense with steam while I stirred and sampled the oozing, bubbling, sugary liquids, and by the time I was done, I had over a dozen jars.

> Every year, as soon as Chris headed north in May, some part of the house demanded attention: the bathtub clogged, the garage got tagged with graffiti, or it rained so much that the lawn sprouted up like a jungle.

When we returned to the city, I looked around our stale apartment—built to resemble a ski chalet too far from anybody's slopes, with faux wood paneling and white carpet—and wondered if I could live without walks through the woods. How could I rejoice in sidewalks and asphalt? Images of the root cellar in my parents' basement, lined with jars of home-canned peaches, tomatoes and apricots, flashed into my mind. I remembered standing in my mother's kitchen as a young girl, watching as she carefully lowered packed jars of tomatoes into an enamel pot of boiling water, knowing they would return to the kitchen in winter as stewed tomatoes, ruining a perfectly good plate of homemade macaroni and cheese. But I had since developed a taste for tomatoes. Maybe canning was just what I needed.

This year, the enamel pot came to a boil in the tiny kitchen of our one-and-half story bungalow. Empty jars floated and bumped into each other in the surge of the water as I waited for them to become sterile, peering through the steam on the windows at Chris ripping tendrils of runaway strawberries out of the garden. He yanked with the vibrant energy we'd both had in June, when we'd confined the strawberries to one small patch so they wouldn't take over the basil or the potatoes. It was our first summer together since we bought the house three years earlier; Chris had finally quit working at camp and joined me in the city full time. We had already started counseling and it had felt hopeful to dig in the dirt together.

I pulled a jar from the boiling water and set it on the counter, where it steamed and dried instantly. I measured a teaspoon of salt and lemon juice into the jar, and its heat released their acrid smell, an odor I have come to recognize as the arrival of fall. I quartered a skinned tomato from the pile on the cutting board and slipped the pieces into the jar, gently mashing them down to release air pockets. Amber tomato juice spilled over the sides of the jar and onto the counter. Six more jars to fill, then back into the water bath for forty-five minutes to seal the lids. Noon had come and gone, and there would be at least two more batches. Tomato pulp and seeds dotted the floor, tomato juice had dried to the counter. The weekend was already spent, and I would barely leave the kitchen.

Every year, as soon as Chris headed north in May, some part of the house demanded attention: the bathtub clogged, the garage got tagged with graffiti, or it rained so much that the lawn sprouted up like a jungle. Two passes with the reel mower resulted in nothing more than a lawn with a bad haircut.

"You just have to keep the grass short, then a reel mower works fine," Chris told me over the phone.

"So you don't think mowing the lawn three times a week sounds like too much?"

He didn't respond the way I wanted him to, by saying he would come home to visit more often, to mow the lawn or pick out a new mower with me.

"We're wasting our summers. We're young. We should be spending them on the road somewhere, traveling, doing things."

Chris' answer was always the same: "Next summer."

I hung up the phone, stepped out onto the back stoop, and looked over at the retired neighbor's perfectly manicured grass to the dandelions growing up around our compost and the long strands of grass at the base of the crab apple tree. I sighed and let my gaze wander to the vegetable garden. A small purple flower on the dark green potato plant caught my eye; it hadn't been there the day before. And a tiny green tomato had popped up during the night, too. I rooted through the garden with the same sense of suspense I felt opening the weekly delivery of produce from the farm share. What new food would I find? Over the summer, I learned that the fennel that looked like fat celery could be roasted to mute its licorice flavor, that eggplant grilled in olive oil kept it from turning into a mushy mass of slime, and that kale was perfect sautéed in garlic. Only okra left me bewildered.

Every time I ate, I savored the knowledge that the basil came from the backyard, the corn had come from the farm an hour away, and the bread from the farmer's market. Each bite felt like a thread that connected me to another person or part of nature, and I grew a new sense of home. But there was one part I didn't like: sitting down to eat at an empty table. In Chris' absence, I made pesto, and blanched green beans, and oven-dried tomatoes. I slid them into the freezer so I could carry that sense of place into winter, when I could extend that thread to my husband and enfold him in the web of connections I had found.

When I lined the jars up on the counter, sunlight streamed through the window and lit their juices like jewels. If all had gone well, I would begin to hear the soft pop of first one jar and then another as a vacuum formed inside, the button center of the metal lid sucking down tight as the seal formed. The sound had become a sound of satisfaction, and this year, a sound of hope. Maybe they could become more than a buoy against the fading temperatures; maybe this year they could provide a buoy for me.

My energy was fading. I had stopped tending the strawberries. Using up the food from the farm share felt like a chore. I mowed the lawn only once, in spite of the new electric mower. We had discussed my growing weariness in counseling. Had started talking about building dreams that grew beyond the edge of the yard, about actually taking the next summer off and letting someone else mow the lawn. There was still hope that in January, Chris might pull a jar down from the cupboard, his pent-up energy from a day in the office spilling out into the kitchen as he bounced around making chili. We might talk about our days and wonder what to do with the coming weekend, make plans for the summer. The thread between us could hold strong.

As the seals started popping, Chris came inside and put his arms around me. "Fun!" he said, looking at the jars. We stood that way for a moment, and then he went back outside.

I hauled the enamel pot off of the stove, propped it on the edge of the kitchen sink and poured out the tarnished, pale brown water. Flecks of swirling tomato pulp streamed into the sink as steam rose up from its surface. I turned my cheek from the heat, glad that my work was

If all had gone well, I would begin to hear the soft pop of first one jar and then another as a vacuum formed inside, the button center of the metal lid sucking down tight as the seal formed. The sound had become a sound of satisfaction, and this year, a sound of hope.

done. Of the seventeen glass jars, three failed to seal. I placed them in the refrigerator, wondering what had been different about those three in particular. What had caused them to fail.

Chris stood by the stove putting leftovers into Tupperware. It was early December, and the leaded panes of the storm window behind him along with the early descent of night obscured the view of the yard. I sat silent at the table. Our dream of an Alaskan canoe trip, one we had actually started planning, had just been snuffed over a dinner out of a box. We were rushing to eat before a holiday party, and the words had come out of his mouth with a strong dose of disbelief, like I was crazy for thinking it could still happen: "There's no way we're going on a canoe trip this summer. Not with the basement renovation."

He snapped the lid on the Tupperware and put it into the fridge. "This is life. A house and a mortgage. We can't do it all." I knew what he really meant. I had heard his implication the week before, from Chris and the therapist, at our final counseling session: It was time to grow up. To be content with what I had.

His logic was sound. A simple repair job had turned the basement into a major renovation. But we had never talked about it as an either/or, and I had thought the basement could wait. I had inhaled sharply when the words flew out of his mouth, ready to argue. But then I thought of all the times I'd heard 'next summer' or 'it just isn't good timing,' how we kept putting off all the dreams that mattered most to me. I knew with a sharp and painful certainty that it would always be this way. I could argue and push for this dream, but only if I was ready to keep doing it, every year, for every dream after that. We would always be waiting, he and I. Like I had waited for him to want to come home during the summer and he now waited for me to be content. We would always be waiting to want the same thing.

It is January now. I go from work to my parents and their kitchen. I think of the tomatoes collecting dust in their cupboard and of Chris living in a house too big for one person; I hope he is taking the time to eat. I mourn the loss of those January dinners, just as I mourn the loss of my tomatoes. My parents have asked: "Why don't you bring them here? Cook with them in our kitchen?" And I could. Instead of wondering if the future will include a place for canning, instead of debating whether preserving tomatoes is worth the effort for a pot of soup for one, I could uncoil the thread to my parents. And maybe bringing those tomatoes out of the cupboard would remind me of summer and the renewal that comes to those who have the patience to see the long winter through.

But to go back to the house that stopped feeling like mine the moment I left, to pull down the jars and pack them in a box… it would give me no delight. I would not think of one last stroll through the market. I would stand on a stool, hold a jar absentmindedly over the refrigerator and look out the kitchen window at the snow-covered yard. I would remember my husband clearing the garden while I covered the windows in steam, and I would marvel at how decisively the threads between us had broken.

Sometimes, the process of preserving does not work. Sometimes, the seals don't form. ✻

Growing Locally

Getting Creative with Community Gardening

by Larry Stebbins, Director, Pikes Peak Urban Gardens

In the winter of 2007 Pikes Peak Urban Gardens (PPUG) was born. It began with an idea I had to help our region build more community gardens (at the time, our city of over 400,000 had only three). My vision was to do just as others have done; find land and a water source, organize the community, and then stand back and watch the veggies grow. Well, I was in for a surprise. Land with water is scarce here, and our hungry urban deer need to be fenced out.

Money to get all this and more would be our first need. I became very familiar with the grant writing process. Four years and 15 grants later, we now have nine more community gardens, a one-half acre demonstration veggie garden and a school greenhouse. If you think it sounds like we drifted from our mission to just build community gardens, you're right. We realized along the way that our mission has really been about teaching folks how to garden in order to grow their own food and providing the resources to get it done.

Community garden projects come in many shapes and sizes. For example, I received a call three years ago from Father Anthony at Holy Theophany Church. He wanted to help open up part of his church property as a garden for his neighbors. PPUG brought soil and building materials for raised beds, some vegetable seeds and seedlings. Today it is a thriving garden with over a dozen families participating. Delicious potluck garden dinners are an added bonus. PPUG was also asked by our city's Parks and Recreation to see if we wanted to help improve underused areas in some of the parks with urban gardening. We jumped at the chance. Our first endeavor was Dorchester Park located in a soon-to-be revitalized business section of our town. There are no homes close to this park, but nearby is the Springs Rescue Mission, an organization that helps rehabilitate recovering men. Together we applied for funds. Today, on about 5,000 square feet of land, some of the men are growing tasty, nutritious food.

It is not a secret that Colorado Springs, like many cities, is experiencing some budget difficulties. The schools are not immune to this problem. As a result a westside elementary school was closed. Today, with the help of PPUG, it hosts a community center, food pantry, and, yes, a community garden. But this is no ordinary garden. The site is an old playground with gravel as deep as you can dig. Our solution was to build up. There are now over 70 raised bed gardens filled with rich organic soil. Some are 30 inches high and only three feet across for our elderly and disabled folks. One gardener in a wheel chair told me that this was the best garden she has ever had.

Our latest project is managing a 42-foot-diameter, off-the-grid, biodome greenhouse at Galileo School of Math and Science in Colorado Springs. We were asked to manage and grow organic salad greens for the students of District 11. This was the brain-child of Rick Hughes, director of Food Services. Jamie Oliver would be proud of how he is changing what the children eat. Fresh, organic, local food is his goal.

Our most ambitious project is our Demonstration Organic Vegetable Garden located on four acres in Colorado Springs. The front acreage is tilled and in production. All summer long, families come to just explore and taste (tasting is encouraged and is free!). If a visitor wants to take home a bunch of lettuce, carrots, cucumbers, or squash there is a small charge. In the Children's Garden each child is allowed to pick a free rainbow carrot. They might get a red, orange, yellow, purple or white one. It is fun to see the little ones walking around munching.

Looking back, if PPUG had just stuck to building "traditional" community gardens, we would be missing many opportunities to help our community become more food self-sufficient. So if you have a community that wants to garden, please think outside the box!

The Garden Club

By Michael Stusser

Illustration by Karley Ford

It started about eight or nine years ago when Brooke, the little girl next door, began yelling at me from her porch.

"That's a hydrangea," she'd shout as I slaved in the yard. "Robins use them to decorate their nests." "If you put that there it won't get any sun." "Those are seeds. If you shove a couple in the ground, they'll come up all over." Gardening was supposed to be a solitary opportunity to concentrate on Mother Nature's wonders; instead, I was being bellowed at by a nine-year-old Master (Sergeant) Gardener.

Brooke had watched me pull weeds, sneeze up a storm and attempt to kill my lawn for years. Eventually she mustered the courage to walk through the hedge that conveniently separates our properties and make additional inane observations, but at much closer range. Pointing out particularly colorful butterflies or helping untangle a hose, Brooke was just helpful enough to keep me from shooing her off the lot.

"I think we should start a Garden Club," she mentioned one day. "Can you make a meeting on Saturday?"

I told her I like to keep my weekends kinda wide open, mainly so I can sleep in. But this was a particularly persistent sprite.

"How about noon?"

I finally relented.

"That's a lot of sleeping. See ya there!" The meeting was set.

* * *

At precisely twelve, Brooke skipped over and plopped down on an overturned pot. I reclined next to her on a lawn chair with an iced espresso in hand. Like a seasoned Shriner, she immediately took charge of the meeting. We proceeded to take a roll call (my idea), discussed some rules (mandatory attendance), and elect a President (she won unanimously). We talked about what flowers we liked, why spiders don't make their webs higher off the ground, and the seminar (thankfully) seemed pretty much over when Brooke demanded we end with a closing ceremony: "Take this dandelion, and I'll take this one. OK – now blow it really hard and make a wish – which you have to tell me!" My first impulse had to do with the lotto, but I substituted it for a prayer that this little person keep her positivity for years to come. Brooke's wish: that we keep the Garden Club meetings going – "Till infinity!"

"Infinity," I echoed. "That's a very long time.

"Well," she replied, "this garden's not going to take care of itself!"

The next few weeks went by without a meeting (rain delays and several hangovers prevented me from toiling in the yard…). One day, on my way to putting out the recycling (she had the schedule down pat), Brooke pinned me for the following Saturday. This time the President was prepared: we had roll call, discussed the state of the garden (pretty good, but my lawn refused to die), followed by a brief ivy removal project. Then Brooke announced it was time for a neighborhood "walking tour" that would feature a number of local gardens.

I was hesitant. "Ya know Brookers," I began, "my theory is that tall fences make good neighbors." After a long pause she laughed, dismissed my anti-social behavior with an eye-roll, and continued with her grand plan. Taking my hand, we visited several neighbor's yards, and I was introduced to people I'd lived next to for years but never spoken with. (That's actually how I wanted it, but Brooke was breaking down more than a few barriers… and opening me up to the remote possibility that youngsters were more than hyper-active noise machines.) Brooke pointed out features in other gardens that I could incorporate into my own (proper tools, sheds, water features, fruit trees, solar lamps edible herbs, etc.). It was then I realized this child had been studying gardening for years and might be a genuine resource on the subject.

* * *

As time went on, Brooke came up with all sorts of agricultural projects. One day it was taking soil samples: "Not good!" she shouted at the Tupperware test tube. "Too much clay, too many potato bugs." Another day was all about aphid spotting (and killing). Though it made her sad, she sprayed the suckers like Al Pacino in Scarface. (The meetings were not without humor: When pondering the reason aphids seemed only to chow newer leaves, Brooke responded, "You wouldn't eat old chicken.")

Many jobs involved Brooke in a supervisory role—me high on a ladder, or with a power-tool of some sort, her looking on with arched brow. "You know what to do if this goes haywire, right?" I'd ask for the umpteenth time.

"Call 911 if you're unconscious or missing any limbs." Smart kid.

As the seasons turned, the Garden Club grew in membership (we added her Mom—my choice—and some boy named Riley with an encyclopedic knowledge of bugs—eating them—not naming them) and frequency.

Once we even had an emergency meeting to deal with a mole wreaking havoc. Brooke (no surprise) had a solution. The mystical concoction was part Harry Potter, part Mad Max, and as effective as napalm. We mixed sugar, our own hair, leaves, salt, bubble gum (tied in a knot) and one last secret ingredient I promised not to divulge (whiskey) into a large bowl, stirred until disgusting, then dripped the mess into several mole holes. Lo and behold (and I swear this is the truth), a few days later the rodent was found lying on his back in the middle of my lawn. (A crude dissection from Riley proved the gum had done the trick.) Brooke, dismayed we killed Mr. Mole, suggested we lessen the dosage next go-round so he only "gets the message" and moves on to some other neighborhood.

We brought pictures of landscapes from magazines and books (she liked topiaries, I liked lawn chairs), and began trading groundcovers, life philosophies, and making real progress (except in killing the damn lawn…). Often meetings were quick—in between her family outings and my frequent naps. The best meetings had sort of a timeless quality—some digging, some strolling to neighborhood pea patches, some lemonade, some more back-breaking labor.

Today Brooke is almost 18 and not nearly as interested in horticulture as boys, bikes, and books. More often than not I wait, shovel in hand, hoping she'll prance over to impart some much-needed wisdom, energy, and unique perspective on bug-catching, digging in the dirt, and stopping to smell the roses.

I hollered over the hedge the other day about unexplained absences and dwindling Club meetings.

"Oh, sorry, Justin and I went to the park on our bikes…"

I suggested we have a pow-wow the following week.

Not one to shirk her elected responsibilities, Brooke arrived promptly at noon. We elected a new President (apparently the ongoing President can break a tie) and, at Brook's insistence, moved a few ferns to shadier locations. At the end of the meeting, I grabbed two dandelions, and we blew like old times. In the midst of the flying fuzz, I realized that our wishes had now changed places; here's to them both coming true… ✿

Oddly Familiar . . .

The Love Life

of

Common

Brown

Seaweed

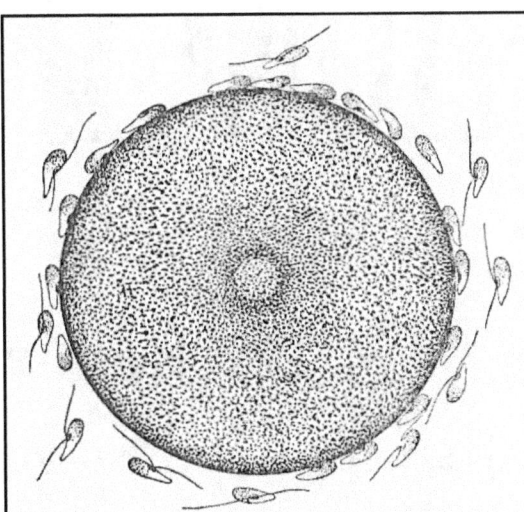

FIG. 216. — An egg cell of Rockweed, surrounded by sperm cells, one of which enters and effects fertilization; × 500. (Redrawn from L. Kny.)

CRUNCHY BETTY

(you have food on your face)

by Leslie Martin

 ## The Honey Challenge

Your Challenge, Should You Choose to Accept It: Wash Your Face with Honey

At first, it was just another food on my face.

Just a sticky-sweet slather of goodness that got rid of pimples, nearly completely erased my scars, and left my skin feeling like a baby's fresh new bottom. But the more I rubbed that gooey, golden nectar over my cheeks, the more real the situation became.

It wasn't just about beating pimples and beauty; it was about an entire circle of creation that existed, in some small way, just to serve my needs. It was earth and rain and flowers and bees, all in a climactic orchestra of perfection that finished with a crescendo on my face. One night, *I got it*. And for as overly dramatic as it sounds, it was good.

And it wasn't just me that got it. Oh no. After finding out how effective it is to wash your face with honey, I submitted a challenge to my blog readers – for two entire weeks, wash your face with honey and water. Period. Over 350 women participated, and the notes **still** come pouring in about how incredible it is.

So I pose the same challenge to all of you: For two weeks, wash your face with honey. Do not skip a day. Notice the difference. And, each time you do, consider the bees. Consider the earth and rain, wind and flowers that all culminated in the moment when you basked in the honey goodness.

Then look in the mirror often, because you're going to love it.

Before you get started with this ultimate honey challenge, though, there are a few things you should know.

Why You Want to Wash Your Face with Honey

1. It is antibacterial and antimicrobial. It will get off any lingering nastiness that's thinking about setting up camp on your face and creating pimples.

2. It is slightly drying which means it helps soak up any pimples or oiliness.

3. It is also incredibly moisturizing. Seems like a double standard, doesn't it? But it's true. Honey sinks into your skin and moisturizes like you wouldn't believe. (Remember Cleopatra and her youthful milk and honey baths?)

4. It imparts beneficial enzymes that work at scrubbing your face for you, as well as perform a little anti-aging action.

5. It's great for acne, aging skin, normal skin, dry skin ... honey loves EVERY SKIN TYPE.

6. It is healing and helps repair acneic sores and scars.

7. It's 100%, absolutely, positively natural, great for your skin, and a simple addition to your beauty routine.

How to Wash Your Face with Honey

These directions are for washing a face that doesn't have makeup on it. Honey alone doesn't take off *all* the goopy gunk. This makes it perfect as your morning facial cleansing agent. And it tastes delicious when you "accidentally" get some on your lips.

Here are your wash instructions:

1. Tie your hair back or get it out of your face. (Honey makes hair really sticky.)

2. Splash your hands and face with just a little water.

3. Pour 1/2-ish teaspoon of honey into the palm of your hands and rub your hands together for 2-3 seconds, just to warm up the honey.

4. Place the honey on your face and massage it in for a minute or two – all around, don't forget an inch of face.

5. Optional – leave the honey sitting there on your face for 5 or 10 minutes, just so your skin can drink the goodness in.

6. Rinse a few times with water. You'll be surprised at how quickly and easily it rinses off!

7. Bask in the **beauty that is now your face**.

Of all things, remember to use raw, unfiltered honey. The kind that comes straight from the bees, not the kind in the store that lacks any pollen whatsoever.

Therein lies your challenge.

If you choose to accept it, I would love to hear about it on Crunchy Betty. Just swing by *www.crunchybetty.com* and leave me a note about how it's worked for you. If you're anything like the hundreds of other women who've recently made the honey switch, you'll love it. And you'll have a brand new appreciation for the bees.

The Garden of Enormous Language

by Carolyn Moore

"One thing about those Olson women: hard-workers, year in and out."
—overheard at the Scholls Grange's Annual Chuckwagon and Craft Bazaar

Olson women worship planting and sausage.
We stuff seeds in casings of moist, spring soil.

In summer, we mothers of gorgeous sweat
water, weed, and hoe all the hot sky long.

We knead allspice, pepper, into raw, chopped meat.
Talk healing. Smear peach pulp on winter aches.

As we heap food on work's altar each fall,
vine maples slough scarlet leaves at our feet.

Rare Breed

by Molly O'Neill

eyond the town of Lindsborg, with its church steeples and 2,000 or so houses, the Kansas prairie is a flat forever. There's nothing to absorb wind or sound. The whinny of gears in a pickup; the bullish snort of a combine harvester turning frosty dirt—the noises of a winter afternoon seem bigger than anything mortal. Standing in a field on Frank Reese Jr.'s farm outside town as the shadows grew longer, I felt truly alone.

I pictured Reese, a poultry breeder who was born near here, shepherding his turkeys across this same, endless horizon as a boy and wondered whether he too had felt alone. From an early age, he had the job of ushering birds on his family's farm from the barn to the open range so that they could peck for insects. He took to the role, and to the birds. When the other children in his first-grade class wrote adoring sonnets to their cats and dogs, Reese crafted a personal essay titled "Me and My Turkeys."

He was surprised by the looks he got. In his young mind, love was love, and he has no memory of not loving turkeys. That is the only way he can explain having devoted his life to preserving the traditional American breeds that were once common on dinner tables across the country. After all, though Reese is a perfectly good cook, he's not the sort of fanatic who'd spend decades chasing the Platonic ideal of an ingredient. He also doesn't seem like the type of person who'd take up the banner against industrial farmer.

BOURBON RED TURKEYS *Poultry Tribune*

In fact, Reese, who is 61 years old, would prefer to spend his evenings reading antique poultry magazines or the spiritual writings of Saint Augustine and Saint Teresa. He is solidly build and speaks in measured tones. In his well-pressed flannel shirt, he looks as if he might have stepped off a page of the 1954 Sears, Roebuck catalogue.

And yet, to food lovers, animal lovers, and many family farmers, this fourth-generation farmer from Kansas is more than just a turkey breeder with old-fashioned ways. He is a saint. Reese is the man who saved American poultry.

From the outside, the farmhouse at the Good Shepherd Turkey Ranch, which is what Reese calls his farm, looks like a monument to a vanished way of life. Set on a corner of the 160-acre spread, the three-story home has Victorian trim and a fresh coat of white paint. It is framed by two red barns and a venerable elm tree, the kind you'd expect to see a swing hanging from. A pie should be cooling on the sill of the kitchen window. Kids should be chasing around the yard.

But Reese is a bachelor. Instead of family portraits and Norman Rockwell prints, turkey-related art hangs on the walls alongside his collection of religious art and blue ribbons from poultry shows. The house is well tended —Reese restored the white pine woodwork and ordered burgundy-colored Victorian-style wallpaper from the designer wallpaper company Bradbury & Bradbury for the dining room and sitting room—but the scent of diesel fuel and turkey coop from Reese's work clothes laces the air. Feed catalogues, fan letters, tax forms, utility bills, and photographs of turkeys are arranged in neat piles on the dining-room table. I'd spent the day visiting the farm with Reese, and he'd invited me in from the cold. The house was utterly quiet but for the sound of the farmer riffling through the papers on the table. Finally, finding what he was after, he waved a black-and-white portrait of a handsome Bronze turkey. "Charlie!" he exclaimed.

"Out of a thousand turkeys," Reese said, "there is always one who wants to be with you all the time. Charlie was my first. When I was a kid, the neighbor's dog got his tail. The vet took one look and said, 'You better just butcher him.' I went nuts and said, 'You fix him!' So he sewed his tail back on, and Charlie and I hung out for the next ten years."

For decades, Reese assumed that he'd gotten so friendly with turkeys when he was a kid merely to make the best of a frustrating situation. "I was the youngest and too little to drive the tractor or handle the cattle or pigs," he said, "so I got sent to the poultry house." Eventually, though, he came to the awareness that there had to be more to it than that. "My father once said that he took me to the state fair when I was three and that all I wanted to do was drag him through the turkey exhibits," Reese told me. "So maybe I was just born this way."

Until he'd grown enough to manage turkeys on his own, Reese showed chickens. He took his first blue ribbon at the Saline County Fair when he was eight years old and won every year for the next decade. Starting at the age of ten, he showed turkeys too.

WHITE HOLLAND TURKEYS

Poultry Tribune

"I got beat a lot," he said. "Back then, there was no kids' division and I was up there showing with all the old, legendary turkey breeders: Norman Kardosh and his Narragansetts, Sadie Lloyd and her Bourbon Reds, Cecil Moore and his Bronzes." The older turkey breeders may have taken home the blue ribbons, but they also took note of Reese's talent. These farmers and enthusiasts had spent lifetimes preserving American barnyard breeds, some of whose bloodlines could be traced to the 1890s. Until Frank Reese appeared, none of those breeders had anointed an heir to continue their legacy. Each knew the clock was ticking.

Growing up, Reese was never more in his element than he was at poultry shows. These bustling events, which took place across rural America throughout the 20th century (and still do, in some areas), culminated in big annual national competitions, where farmers and hobbyists displayed prized birds that they'd bred for hardiness, meat quality, reproductive prowess, and physical beauty. Held in vast exhibition halls, the juried contests were similar to dog shows, a Best in Show milieu in which hair dryers were aimed at feathers rather than fur. "If you won the national show, you were set because everybody wanted to buy your birds," said Reese.

The shows were also where older breeders mentored potential successors. "They taught me the breed history," Reese remembered. "They had me sitting on the ground with my standards book, studying each bird." Reese was talking about Standards of Perfection, a guide published by the American Poultry Association that recognizes eight distinct varieties of turkey that are considered to be the purest farm breeds and describes the ideal physical characteristics of each one. The book, first published in 1874, harks back to an era when the difference between common breeds of chickens and turkeys were as dramatic as the differences between, say, a Great Dane and a Dachshund. These varieties were raised for different uses: big roasters for Sunday dinners, tough and flavorful stewers for soups, plump-legged fryers, and so on.

Norman Kardosh, a breeder from Alton, Kansas, was Reese's most influential teacher. "Norman taught me about the importance of fine breeding, how it ensures the survival of the best bloodlines and how that, in turn, ensures biodiversity among the species. Without those two things, any creature is doomed to extinction."

At some point in the late 1970s, after earning a nursing degree and finishing a stint in the army in Texas, Reese realized that standard bred birds—as the types of poultry recognized in Standard of Perfection are called—were in trouble. He was raising turkeys at his home south of San Antonio and competing on the side. "I'd always competed against 50 to 100 birds at every show. Suddenly it was just me," he recalled.

American farmers just weren't raising standard bred birds anymore, at least not in significant numbers. "The commercial industry had developed a couple varieties that cost less to feed, fattened up faster, and sold well, and farmers raised these to the exclusion of all others," Reese explained to me. "This means that one flue could wipe out every bird in this country." To make matters worse, he said, commercial birds—a broad-breasted white variety developed in the 1950s—all tend to taste the same. "They have no flavor! No individuality!" he lamented.

Reese began expanding his flock. Meanwhile, he worked as a nurse at a hospital in San Antonio and eked out additional money by taking odd jobs and even modeling. In his early 30s, Reese looked every inch the Marlboro Man, whom he once portrayed in an advertising campaign.

Texas was fun, said Reese, "but it was no place to raise a turkey." So, in 1989, he moved back to Kansas, bought a farm outside Lindsborg that he called Good Shepherd Turkey Ranch, and ramped up his breeding program. He was more worried than ever about American poultry. "The bloodlines were dying out. Norman didn't want to believe me," Reese recalled. "He was in his late 70s, but he got in his truck and went looking for his birds. He went to every farm he'd sold to, and he didn't find one Norman Kardosh Narragansett." Reese's other mentors were beginning to pass away. Norman was the last to go," Reese said, "I promised him that I would not let these birds die off the face of the Earth."

By 2002, Reese had increased the national population of standard bred turkeys to such an extent that he was able to sell to some restaurants and individuals. "The only way to save these birds is to get people to eat them," he said. Reese created a cooperative of several farmers in Kansas and sold 800 heritage turkeys--as the farmers branded their standard bred birds--that first year. Two years later, Reese took on a business partner, a young poultry farmer named Brian Anselmo, whom Reese considered to be the next heir to the old-breed poultry legacy. In 2007, the number of farmers in the Good Shepherd co-op grew to a dozen; they sold 10,000 old-breed turkeys that Thanksgiving. It wasn't much compared with the 46 million industrially raised turkeys sold during that holiday each year, but it was a milestone nonetheless.

In 2008, Anselmo died suddenly of complications of asthma at the age of 28. Reese, recognized by then as the premier source of old-breed birds in the nation, became even more focused on selling his breeding stock. "I'm all these birds have now," Reese said. Nowadays, he's pouring his energy into plans for the Standard Bred Poultry Institute, a place where farmers will learn how to breed, raise, preserve, and cook these birds. He is building on the facility, using his own savings, and, he hopes, donor money, on the ridge just beyond his barns. "I'm leaving it all to them," Reese said.

Poultry Tribune

BRONZE TURKEYS

We'd been sitting in his dining room for a long while. Outside, the wind was keening around the house. Reese pushed back from the table, and I followed him as he walked to the kitchen, zipped a barn jacket over his flannel shirt, pulled on a stocking cap, and walked out his back door.

We headed toward the pasture next to the larger of the two red barns. There, under a darkening sky, hundreds of turkeys were already crowding at the fence, strutting excitedly, puffing their feathers, and craning their wobbly-skinned necks. The birds mobbed Reese as he pushed through the gate. At the center of this shiny, feathery universe, Reese chattered and scolded. Bending down, he scooped up a huge Bronze and cradled it in the crook of his arm.

"This is Norman," he said, beaming. The bird had bright eyes and copper-colored feathers with black edges. He put Norman down, and the animal spread its lush tail feathers in an impressive rainbow. "Isn't he something?" said Reese. "We've been hanging around for a few years. Norman isn't going anywhere. Norman's staying right here." ❋

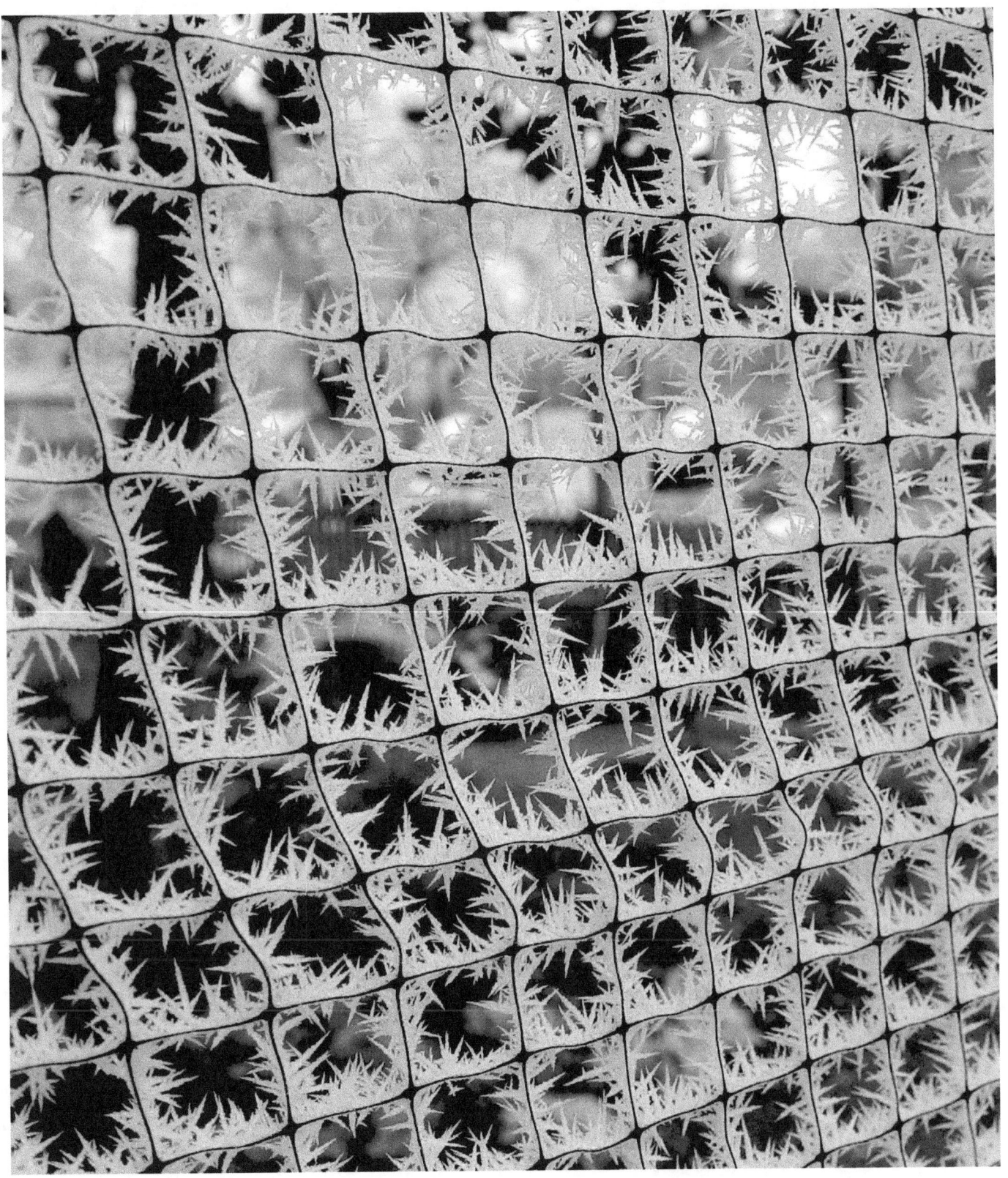

Hoarfrost Fence

by Kim Gravestock

Winter Dream with Garden
by
Carolyne Wright

I

Always the sensation of new life
riding through forests with the windows
down, remote mansions flickering
like candles through the trees.
We surge with Christmasses.

II

A branch breaks off. Green veins
bleed into air. All the passers-by
in the garden pause, a sudden
frost of a stare. A late pear
lets go of its stem, its bruising
plump in turf muffled.
The scene turns over like a leaf
before it falls, sleepers
almost awakening. Their hearts—
stone gardens raked by stooped,
obedient man at dawn.

III

Traffic at a distance mimics geese, slow
wheeling around of the long flocks.
Pale green pries through our lids.
We turn under the heaped snow
of the blankets, searching again
in the back alleys of sleep
for wind that whistles thinner
as if through a shrinking reed.
Dreams recede, kettles ringing
at winter's borders, stones
over old ice that skip and startle
before they plunge. Our lids
fly up, alarmed. That's all. Morning
comes into focus on the wall.

Pulsatilla Vulgaris - Pasque Flower
by Benjamin Vogt

Kim Gravestock

In April fingered leaves reach up like praying hands, and from their centers an oval of dark magenta rises covered in peach fuzz. The stem too, thick and short, seems to be covered in a white halo, as if emerging from a bed of frost. The thin petals unfurl, dark purple, at the center a gumdrop of yellow stamens. And there, at the center of the center, a wild explosion of purple like a frozen mushroom cloud, the style, an echo of the flower's rising, the petals unfurling. Everything about this is chilled, preserved, a bridge between the cold nights and suddenly warm days. Every new bud breaking ground seems awkward and unsure, even premature. They keep low, careful to not leave the safety of the warming soil. In the evening the only sign that there was a flower is the gathering together of soft tentacles to preserve the next day's resurrection. ❀

March Equinox
by
J. D. Smith

Quiescent seed, round bulb and corm
Stay bound until the hard fields warm
And let potential rise to form,
Defined, in turn, by drought and storm.

Rachael Davis

"Clethra" —from TheGraphicsFairy.com

Name that Sprout!

Test your horticultural acumen by matching the sprout to the plant.

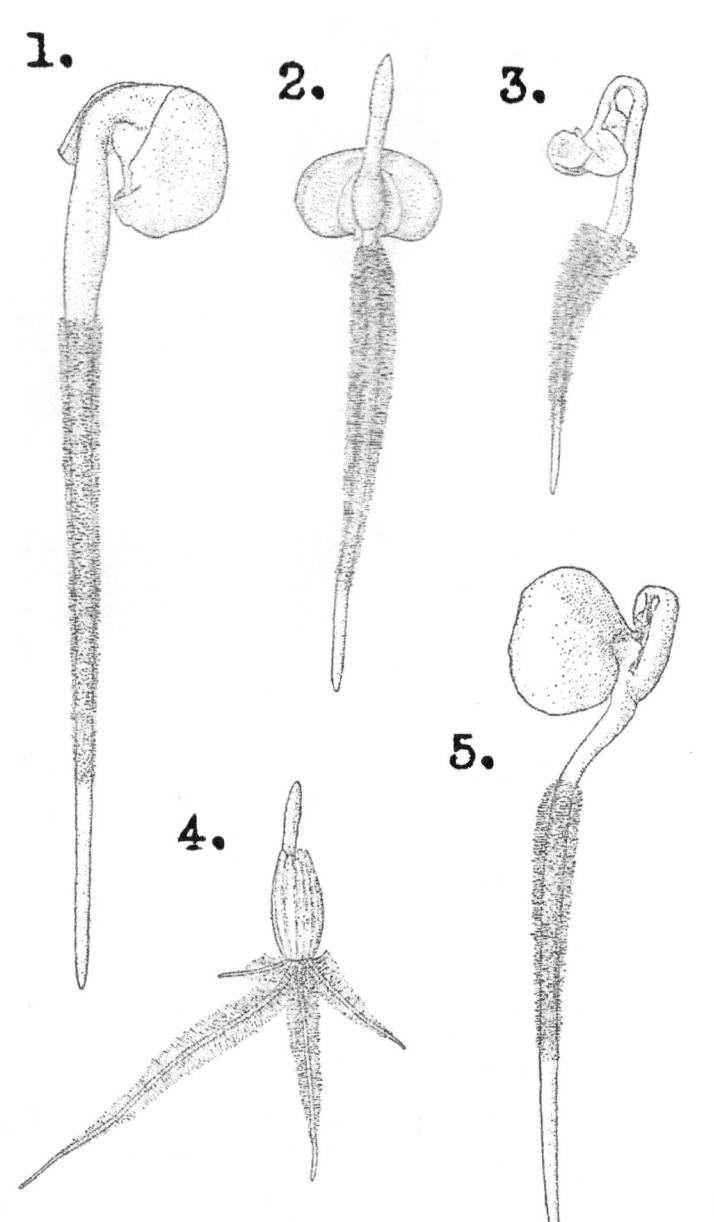

A. Lupine
B. Radish
C. Pea
D. Oats
E. Corn

Illustrations from *A Text-Book of Botany for Colleges*, 1917.

Sadie & Ruby ♥ Greenwoman Magazine

Sadie: My mind's still reeling from the thought-provoking articles and stories I read last night.

Ruby: Mine too! *Greenwoman*'s a great mind trip.

Sadie: Can't wait for the next volume. . .

Ruby: Neither can I.

Let's Stay in Touch!

FREE download when you sign up!

We can do just that if you sign up for our weekly newsletter at www.greenwomanmagazine.com.

Available through Amazon.com (if that's how you roll).

In return, we'll send you garden writing fabulousness, special offers on our books, and more!

Or Read Online (the greenest option) for only $2.95 an issue!

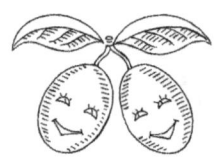

In the Produce Aisle

by Mae Fayne and Angus Skillet

Darling, all I ask is that you promise me we'll be able to avoid a stew.

Wilson A. Bentley

350 SCIENCE
THE BASICS OF CLIMATE CHANGE SCIENCE

There are three numbers you need to really understand global warming: 275, 389, and 350.

For all of human history until about 300 years ago, our atmosphere contained 275 parts per million (ppm) of carbon dioxide. That's a useful amount—without some CO_2 and other greenhouse gases that trap heat in our atmosphere, our planet would be too cold for life on Earth.

About 300 years ago, humans began to burn coal and oil to produce energy and goods. The amount of carbon in the atmosphere began to rise. By doing everyday activities like cooking, or turning on the lights, we're taking millions of years worth of carbon, stored beneath the earth as fossil fuels, and releasing it into the air. At the same time, we're changing the way we use our land, cutting down trees and tilling our farmland, which also adds CO_2 to our atmosphere.

By now—and this is the second number—the planet has 389 parts per million CO_2 – and this number is rising by about 2 ppm every year.

PARTS PER MILLION (PPM)

The concentration of CO_2 in our atmosphere is measured in "parts per million", which simply means a ratio of CO_2 molecules per million molecules in our atmosphere. There's currently 389 parts per million (ppm) in the atmosphere. 389ppm may sound like a small amount, but our atmosphere is so finely tuned that changing this concentration just a little bit can disrupt our entire planet.

Climate Change Impacts

In the last few years, it's become clear that the rise of CO_2 in our atmosphere is having an effect much faster and more severely than scientists once predicted. Here are a few examples of impacts we're already seeing:

Sea Levels are Rising: Scientists warn they could go up several meters this century, threatening the homes of hundreds of millions of people.

Glaciers are Melting: They're disappearing fast— and glaciers are the only source of drinking water for hundreds of millions of people.

Oceans are Acidifying: Warmer and more acidic oceans are killing a vast amount of the world's coral reefs.

Weather is More Severe: Hurricanes, typhoons and droughts are becoming more frequent, harsher, and unpredictable.

Mosquitoes are Spreading: They're thriving in new places, and are bring malaria and dengue fever with them.

Impacts are speeding up

The Arctic is sending us the clearest message that climate change is happening now, and much faster than scientists once thought. In the summer of 2007, the extent of Arctic sea ice decreased by nearly 40%. It is melting so fast that scientists now believe the Arctic could have no ice in the summertime as early as 2013, which is 80 years ahead of what had been predicted just a few years ago.

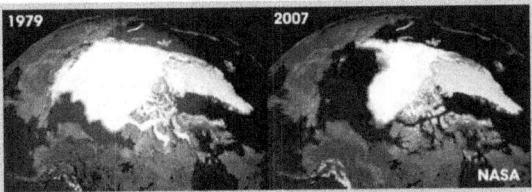

350ppm: The safe level of CO_2 for our atmosphere

350 parts per million is the third and final number to remember, and it represents the safety zone for planet Earth. Above 350ppm we risk reaching dangerous 'tipping points' (see right). We don't know how long

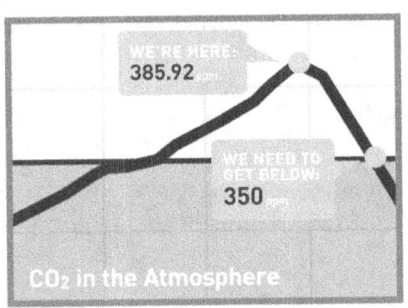

we can stay above 350ppm—this number is far outside the range we've seen in our recorded history— but we do know that the smart thing would be get back to the safety zone as soon as possible.

What's a "Climate Tipping Point"?

This means a point in time when the earth's climate begins to change in ways we can't undo in our lifetimes - or possibly for many, many generations. Tipping points are fed by impacts that reinforce each other, called 'feedback loops'. For example, as Arctic sea ice melts, the darker ocean absorbs more sunlight, becomes warmer, and speeds melting. An example of a tipping point, is the potential melting of the Greenland or Antarctic ice sheet. These are dangerous events that we must avoid by getting below 350ppm as soon as possible.

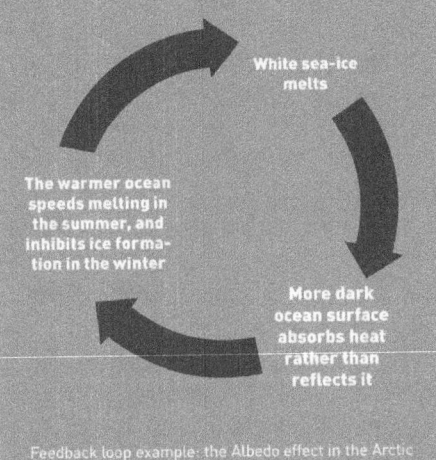

Feedback loop example: the Albedo effect in the Arctic

"If humanity wishes to preserve a planet similar to that on which civilization developed and to hich life on Earth is adapted, paleoclimate evidence and ongoing climate change suggest that CO_2 will need to be reduced from its current 389 ppm to at most 350 ppm."

—Dr. James Hansen, NASA

 350.org

350.org is an international grassroots campaign that aims to mobilize a global climate movement united by a common call to action. By spreading an understanding of the science and a shared vision for a fair policy, we will ensure that the world creates bold and equitable solutions to the climate crisis. 350.org is an independent and not-for-profit project.   Visit www.350.org or contact organizers@350.org to get involved.

Garden Song:
Christa Decicco is a musician who likes to get her hands dirty. by Robin Intemann

erforming 150-plus days a year might be more than enough to thwart most gardeners, but Christa DeCicco, vocalist and songwriter for Christabel and the Jons, still manages to find ways to get her hands dirty.

Growing up in a musical family near the lush flora of the Smoky Mountains helped develop DeCicco's dual passions. She received a received a bachelor's degree in Ornamental Horticulture and Landscape Design from the University of Tennessee in 2003 and maintains her own freelance gardening business as time allows.

DeCicco's voice is often characterized as "velvety," and her original music is described as a diverse blend of folk, jazz, bossa nova, and other styles. Based in Knoxville, Tennessee, DeCicco has performed on national and international stages. Last spring took her on a tour of the Western United States, and in the summer Christabel and the Jons performed in seven states in the south and along the eastern seaboard. In September they headed to the Mediterranean Festival of the Arts in Crete (Greece) and headed back home in October to host DeCicco's own annual festival, The Hilltop Dinner & Dance, in Knoxville.

While DeCicco has been singing and playing music since childhood, Christabel and the Jons was formed in the spring of 2005. Joining DeCicco on vocals and guitar are Seth Hopper on violin, mandolin, trumpet, and accordion, and Jon Whitlock on drums. The band has released three full-length albums: "Love and Circumstances" (2006); "Custom Made For You" (2008); and "The Christmas Album" (2010). Its fourth studio release, "The Same Mistake," is set for release later this year.

We caught up with DeCiccio between gigs and gardening in mid-September.

Greenwoman: You have said that music and gardening are the two greatest interests in your life and you're lucky to be able to do both professionally. (DeCicco has been making a living through her music and landscaping businesses since 2004.) How do they complement one another?

DeCicco: The musician lifestyle and the farmer lifestyle are very different. Doing both helps keep me balanced. They each have busy and slow seasons. Sometimes it's difficult to switch back and forth from a day schedule to a night schedule. And it's a whole different wardrobe. Sometimes people don't recognize me if they're used to seeing me one way and then they see me dressed completely differently for my other job.

Greenwoman: Yes—gardening clothes are quite different from the pretty vintage dresses that you wear on stage. You seem to love vintage, you even play a 1950s Silvertone archtop guitar. Where did that interest come from?

DeCicco: I started buying vintage in high school at flea markets and thrift stores, and I guess I never grew out of it. I like to imagine the story that the clothes would tell about their previous owners: the parties they attended, the drinks that were spilled on them, the weddings and graduation ceremonies they attended, that sort of thing. For stage wear my band likes to look pretty formal, so I go for a lot of 1950s party dresses with tight waists and full skirts. For fun I like 1960s for the crazy prints and bright colors. Crinolines are great, but difficult to drive a car in so I usually carry mine in a bag and put it on at the last minute.

Greenwoman: How did you decide on a degree of horticultural landscape and design?

DeCicco: Ever since I was young I've always enjoyed plants and the studies of biology and ecology. When I was in college I selected that concentration because I wanted a job that allowed me to work outside, was intellectually challenging and engaging, had a beneficial environmental aspect to it, and was a blend of art and science.

Greenwoman: I love it—gardening does have it all. I get the sense that your gardening may be as eclectic as your music. Would you describe your garden?

DeCicco: Since I have always been a renter, I have a very large potted garden that goes with me from house to house. I do my vegetable gardening at a local community garden called Beardsley Community Farm. Inside on my dresser I have a large collection of jades, succulents, and cacti in little vintage McCoy planters. I always plant a few annuals wherever I live because I like to see a little color every day.

Greenwoman: And what are those colorful annuals?

DeCicco: This year, right outside my front door I planted a zinnia 'Cut and Come Again' mixture, nasturtiums, a vitronella-scented geranium, and a moonflower that has wrapped my column and probably grown more than 20 feet! On my porch in pots, I have pink impatiens, blue lobelia, strawberries, Kalanchoe thyrsiflora 'Flapjacks' and other succulents, white Angelonia angustifolia, boston ferns, spearmint, pineapple mint, thyme, a weeping willow, a butterfly bush, and a wisteria. I like to propagate plants from nature or share cuttings from friends. I would have a very different garden if I were not a renter. I would invest in fruit trees (peach, cherry, pear, and apricot) and might even try an espalier. I would also have lots of bulbs, I love how low maintenance they are and how easily they reproduce on their own—especially Easter lilies, 'Casa Blanca' lilies, grape hyacinth, regular hyacinths, 'Pheasant's Eye' daffodils, and Star of Bethlehem. Someday I would like to live on a small farm and produce cut flowers and herbs.

Greenwoman: What's happening this year at the community garden?

DeCicco: In Tennessee we have a long fall growing season so this fall I've replanted a lot of the same crops I grew early this spring. I've planted 'Rainbow' Swiss chard, onions, spinach, red leaf lettuce, arugula, carrots, beets, kale, cilantro, and strawberries. This year I also broke ground near my house and planted a small herb garden of thyme, oregano, Italian parsley and fennel. I really like leafy greens and herbs. In the summer I worship tomatoes and

Photo by Brian Wagner

could eat two to three big ones a day. I'm also a big fan of zucchini, green beans, okra, raspberries, blackberries and peaches.

Greenwoman: Yum! Does living in East Tennessee influence what you do musically as well?

DeCicco: The economy and history of this area are very linked to agriculture. There is also a strong musical tradition here with a lot of different genres overlapping both today and in the past: delta blues, Appalachian old-time traditional fiddle tunes, classic country/honkytonk, gospel, bluegrass, ragtime, swing, jazz, even classical.

Greenwoman: So you've always been into the local traditional music?

DeCicco: When I was a young teenager first discovering music, I was influenced by Joni Mitchell, Bob Dylan, Tori Amos, Ani Difranco, Gillian Welch. Then I went through a stage of listening to a lot of vintage jazz, especially Billie Holiday, Louis Armstrong, Ella Fitzgerald, and Julie London. Now I'm going through a phase of listening to old honkytonk and classic country like Hank Williams, Floyd Tillman, and Bob Wills and the Texas Playboys. When we perform we do about half originals and half covers. Right now I'm really enjoying doing covers of those classic country singers I just mentioned.

Greenwoman: You certainly live a life of creativity. Can you imagine NOT performing or gardening?

DeCicco: No, but I can imagine doing other things. I started my own festival, Hilltop Dinner & Dance, and I'm enjoying all the new and challenging aspects of organizing that project. I love to cook and entertain. Sometimes I daydream of how cool it would be to be a professionally trained chef. I also wouldn't mind being a "kept woman"

so I could just paint and sew and make quilts all day long!

Greenwoman: [Laughs.] The second annual Hilltop Dinner & Dance is scheduled for October. Tell me what that will be like.

DeCicco: I wanted to have an event that would showcase the things I love about living in the South, especially east Tennessee, and bring together my whole community for a big ol' Appalachian-themed party. We have a lot of history and musical and culinary culture here, but not a lot of dancing! People say they are embarrassed by "not knowing how." I really wanted to do something to bring traditional social dancing back to Knoxville. By that I am referring to three types of dances: square dance, two-step, and swing dance. So I choose bands that are highly 'danceable' and I hire dance instructors from the Knoxville Swing Dance Association to teach free beginner lessons between each band. I have an area set up for kids with games and tents in the woods they can romp around in. One of my best friends, Rita Cochran, is doing a full menu of southern food focusing on local seasonal ingredients, complete with her own homemade ice cream. And, yes there are lots and lots of hay bales and fairy lights.

Greenwoman: It's fascinating how gardeners' and artists' work evolves. It seems like your evolution has taken you back to your roots—pun intended.

DeCicco: I have evolved as a musician from wanting to travel and see the world to wanting to create something lasting and positive in my hometown. I hope that Hilltop will become my signature event, maybe even my legacy.

For more information about Christabel and the Jons visit http://christabelmusic.com/

Winter's Heart
by Elisabeth Kinsey
(a Sex in the Garden Essay)

Rachael Davis

In the heart of winter, I contemplate my winter's heart. Frigid days bring sinking into slush puddles against the icy wind, starting the day with cold feet, jumping into a dark car only to join the cattle call of the highway. I have to refuse this heart. My heart is elsewhere. I am consumed by the memory of a rose.

Take a rose petal in your hand. Stroke it. Lift it to your cheek. Are you transported to Juliet's attempt at scooping with her tongue the last drops of poison from the bottle lying atop her still warm Romeo's body? Do you float somewhere between the trilled and gasping aria in *Rigoletto*? Are you reminded of a warning not to pursue someone because they'd destroy your life à la a Thomas Hardy novel character?

My education on rose sensuality began at the mall. "Grasse, France, the perfume capital of the world" began a video clip educating the masses on how enticing and special are David Austin roses and the perfumeries distilling their elegant nectars. The woman in the video had a husky British voice and her words about petals unfolding scent transported me from a slushy snow world into the Northern California spring I danced in as a child. I was in love. And it wasn't the fickle love of first dates, that front seat cranked down and tongue going in all directions that I had experienced too much of the time. My love for the English rose bloomed into a full-on obsession. I didn't just need this perfume, or to get my hands on this rose—I needed the rose to need me.

That next spring, the smell of apricots, as if each petal were dipped in elixir, quivered and released in the air around me when I found the David Austin 'Evelyn' rosebush at a local nursery. Instead of the shaft of light that translates good souls up to heaven, a deep tunnel opened in the earth on the way to my carnal thoughts. I fingered a petal and shrunk away. With an investment of forty dollars and a bloom so tiny, so delicate, I didn't have a clue what I was doing. Could my obsession be lust? Could I be that simpleton who would never get far with the rose?

Before this day, my only encounters with roses had been rough at best. I remembered a feud roses had caused in my youth when my father had the sprinkler going at top speed and our hunched over, cardigan-clad neighbor, Mimi, knocked arthritically, "Tell your father that he's mildewing my roses." (I pictured powdered and petulant pink ladies, wilting in the rain.)

Years later, another rose encounter—a rental where my entire front porch was covered with a faded pink not found in a crayon box. These roses were big, floppy-headed and full of feminine folds. Their scent escaped in tiny rivulets of daintiness. Greedy, I cut them all and floated their tops whole in a bath, felt my skin turn to velvet. I thought I'd get a second chance when the roses re-bloomed. That day never came, the bush being the cottage rose variety, blooming once per summer. I was Alice in Wonderland's Red Queen, who had clipped the floppy heads into extinction. I tried to vindicate myself by purchasing a small thorny and lonely-looking bush which I promptly stuck in a hard-to-dig hole. Thinking I had some inherent rose knowledge, I watered it every day, sprinkled what I thought it needed, coffee grounds and bone meal. Instead of growing up and out, it shriveled and shrunk into the ground.

I was undeserving of the Rose's love, a burly slut to its very delicate nature. I left 'Evelyn' at the altar and made for the library. There I took out books on roses, to get past my realization of simple lust. Obsessed with the thought of growing a David Austin rose, I studied them, discovering that they are tea roses bred to be hearty but that they still needed delicate cajoling. On the website I read, "In the 1940s...The Old Roses—that is the Gallicas, Damasks, Albas, etc.—had all but died out...His [David Austin's] objective being to create new roses in the style of Old Roses, thus combining the unique charm and fragrance of Old Roses with the wide colour range and repeat-flowering qualities of Modern Roses." I began to understand; although they claimed a hearty history, they still needed some one-on-one time. My sloppy first attempt was the equivalent of that first groping date. If I wanted quality, I'd have to spend some time and money, wine and dine. Roses needed my romance.

I learned that gently soaking the bare root-rose (many roses are offered through catalogues in this state) before planting will improve its chances for commitment to soil. I don't mind saying that a little Barry White, moonlight, a good Chianti and a Black Forest torte might also help. Next, make sure your soil is loose with desire, and loose enough to drain throughout the seasons. You can overwater and come on too strong. Their dusky natures need six hours of sun, at the very least, says the AARS (All American Rose Society). On a forum discussing roses, one San Franciscan commented, "Roses often have a reputation of being fussy, but I think that's only true if you are fussy over them. They're actually pretty easy to grow and are one of the few things that have really taken root in my sandy garden. Just buy a bunch of lady bugs to keep the aphids off and you'll be fine." Wha? What about those of us who have to cover our tomatoes near the end of fall because hail will rip anything left off a vine? The time to think about lady bugs is after winning the rose's heart. I still needed to order my bush.

Catalogues galore and the David Austin website open, I decided that I was ready to commit. The day I ordered my rosebush was the worst snow storm a January could offer. As the storm battered my winter's heart, I read up on a 'Jude the Obscure' rose, promising to be "A very strong, unusual and delicious fragrance with a fruity note reminiscent of guava and sweet white wine. Pleasing medium yellow on the inside of the petals and a paler yellow on the outside." I had studied that Hardy novel for its characters' poor choices, because in the writing world we have to push our characters into peril, so that when and if they are saved, it is so sweet to the reader. (By the way, you need a strong constitution to read this book, or just hide the knives, as it is Hardy's most dark and tragic.)

On a happy spring day when the morning doves started to coo on my front porch, Jude was delivered. I dug a big enough hole, sifting compost and my sandy earth together, and then helped him down. That summer, I learned the art of pruning, taking care of root drainage, and that watering is a delicate science. When sunflowers took over my garden is when Jude opened up into a first pink-colored, then after a full day of sun, bleaching out to a light pinky-white fat and foldy face.

Now that I've planted a 'Sir Thomas Lipton'(one stem of the creamy-white blossoms will perfume an entire room), a day-glow orange rose bush called "Treasure Orange," that snagged my scan at a garden center, and Hardy's most tragic Austin, 'Jude', I know what it is like to love deeply, after lust recedes. Roses will honor us with their giving natures, but only if we give them what they need. They hold all the petals, like answers, close to their hearts.

References:
Austin, D. (2011). History of David Austin Roses. Retrieved on 9.15.2011. www.davidaustenroses.com.
Apartment Therapy. (2008). Roseslaw comment. Retrieved on 9.15.2011. www. apartmenttherapy.com.

Swarm Story

by Sandra Knauf

ony kept calling me Marsha.

"Look over here, Marsha," he beckoned. My attention was fixed on the activity going on above my head so I didn't look over until he called again. Then it dawned on me—he thought *I* was Marsha. I understood the mistake. Although he'd helped me dress just a few minutes ago, he didn't know me. We'd just met the night before.

I turned on the ladder where I balanced seven feet up underneath a white pine. I looked down. The wind blew slightly, cool and crisp, typical for a April morning in front range Colorado.

A few feet above my head hummed a swarm of five thousand bees.

I smiled down at Tony, even though it wouldn't show, from behind the veil. Tony took my picture.

* * *

I've always liked insects, and bees are a favorite—they're attractive, industrious and socially complex, they live in amazing hive-cities, and they create one of nature's most perfect, delicious foods. While I'm not a beekeeper yet, my curiosity and obsession with gardening has been leading me in that direction. Just the spring before, for fun and education, I'd attended a Beginning Beekeeping class, held by the Pikes Peak Beekeepers Association. The two days of instruction covered everything from bee anatomy to honey extraction, but what really made my antennae stand up was the session on swarm capture. From what I learned, capturing a swarm of bees was a profitable, nearly risk-free venture—and as easy as stealing candy from a baby.

* * *

A jolly, bearded, ursine man by the name of Mike presented the session.

"The primary reason swarming occurs is overcrowding," he said. "To keep the hive healthy and to increase their population elsewhere, they divide."

He went on to explain that they begin the process by producing a new queen for the existing hive. The nurse bees feed a few of the larvae royal jelly, the larvae grow and then soon enter their final metamorphic stage into adulthood. The first queen bee who hatches from this metamorphic stage usually wins, by dispatching of her still-pupating rivals; in fact, a queen's stinger is used only for that purpose. But even before this, the old queen, who first had food withheld from her so she'd stop laying eggs, and then was further harassed by her hive-mates so she'd get down to a trim flying weight, has left with at least half of the hive.

Since it can take several days to find a location for a hive and settle in, the departing bees gorge themselves on honey. They're so stuffed their bodies are taut, making it nigh-impossible for them to curve around and sting. The binge also renders them docile. Usually the swarm will land within one to two hundred feet of the old hive, and they'll hang on a tree or shrub branch together, with the queen protected near the middle, while scout bees make a final decision on their hive location. During a warm period, they release and fly together to the new digs. While the entire process can stretch out over a period of several weeks, the swarming itself usually occurs during a single day.

"All you really need for a capture, if the swarm is in a convenient place, is a couple of cardboard boxes with lids," Mike said. He stroked his dark beard nonchalantly while looking around the class, a diverse group of young, old and middle-aged participants. He savored our surprised expressions. "I use paper boxes, the kind reams of paper come in. You can also use an empty hive super, which is the box-like section of a commercial hive. Of course, any openings have to be duct taped. Then, if the swarm's in a bush near the ground, where it's easily accessible, you can just put the box directly underneath it, give the branch they're hanging on a good jerk, and they fall in." He grinned. "It's like one bee's holding onto the branch and then someone's holding on to him and so on, in a big chain, so when you shake it and the one lets go, they all let go."

Our group chuckles.

"Within a few minutes the remaining bees will form a smaller cluster, so you just have a second box on hand to get those. You can even have a third box, but the bees that are left will return to the hive."

He told how he typically wears only a veil for protection (no gloves or suit) while capturing a swarm. "The bees are sluggish from all that honey," he said, "they're really almost incapable of stinging you."

He talked about bait hives that bee catalogues sell to capture swarms. "They don't really work very well, but I found something that does. It's a huge paper pot with a lid that you hang from a tree with wire. In it you place a lure, artificial queen pheromone, which is also available through the catalogues.

"The scout bees will find the pot and look around for the queen but won't find her. They'll measure the pot, to make sure it's big enough, then they'll report back to the swarm that they've found a home. Two years ago I captured five swarms this way, but when I tried to use the queen pheromone again a year later it didn't work. Apparently it has to be fresh."

Mike said the Beekeepers Association worked with the County Extension Office, the Department of Wildlife and the Humane Society each spring, taking calls from frantic homeowners who discover a swarm on their property and want something done about it—immediately. It doesn't matter that the bees will leave on their own in a day or so at the most, the swarms are perceived as a serious threat. So he or another beekeeper on the "swarm list" go out and capture the bees to add to their own colonies. Mike said it was fun to have people watch, impressed with his apparent bravery.

"One morning I got a call," he told us. "There was a swarm at an elementary school, in a bush near the front door. By the time I got there, they had several classes standing out on the sidewalk to observe. I decided to give them a good show. There I was, standing close to the swarm, showing them my beekeeper's suit, my veil and my gloves, taking my sweet time putting them on, all the while talking about the bees. After I finally dressed, I turned to begin the capture, and the bees," Mike snapped his thick fingers, "took off just like that." He laughed a deep belly-laugh. "I had taken too long. Boy, I can tell you, that was impressive."

By the end of the presentation all I could think was: *This is so cool. I want to capture a swarm of bees.*

* * *

I had to wait another year before I had a chance. The next spring I attended the Pikes Peak Beekeepers Association's meeting. I went knowing it was almost swarm season and the beekeepers would be putting together a swarm list. I wanted to be on that list. The meeting, one of only four each year and the first one I had ever attended, took place at a neighborhood church. After the used beekeeping equipment sale in the parking lot, the thirty to forty members and their guests moved inside. As we settled into our folding chairs, waiting for the meeting to begin, I listened to the two men talking in the row in front of me.

The older of the two, who looked to be in his seventies, was thin and grizzled. He wore loose faded jeans and a worn madras print shirt. "The tree was taken down," he said, in a tone loud enough for surrounding beekeepers to hear, "and about five hundred pounds of honey was recovered."

"Five hundred?" said the man next to him. He was nice looking, neatly dressed, appeared to be in his mid-to-late fifties, just a little younger than my dad. He paused for a moment, considering. "You'd have to scrape it off, then filter it. There'd be a lot of junk in it; dead bees, stuff from the tree."

"One time I captured a swarm in the woods, then found the tree it came from," said the old-timer. "I knocked the tree down, took the rest of the bees and the honey, then cleaned up the honey and fed it back to them."

The buzzing quieted down as the president of the Association opened the meeting. He asked for guests to introduce themselves, and when it when it was my turn I told the group that I was a writer and gardener. I said I had attended the beekeeping class the year before and was interested in observing a swarm capture.

I took my seat and the two men who had been talking turned to me.

The fifty-something man whispered, "There's a swarm by the Country Club. We're going to capture it tomorrow. Do you want to go in the morning, if they're still there?"

"Sure," I answered, stunned by the immediate gratification of my heart's desire. The man introduced himself as Tony and drew a map showing how to get to his house. He said he'd call me by 8 A.M. and let me know if the bees were still there. He said he had a veil I could borrow and instructed me to wear light colored clothing.

* * *

The next morning I awoke early, excited and thinking about the swarm, hoping it was still there. I dressed in khakis, cowboy boots, and a long-sleeved white shirt. In the class we were told beekeepers wear white clothing because bees don't like dark colors; big dark shapes outside of the hive look too much like hungry bears. Moving on with my toilette, I discovered that for deodorant I had only a natural brand, honeysuckle rose scented, or lavender talcum—both no-no's in beekeeping. They'd mentioned this particular commandment in bee school as well. Do not perfume thyself before bee handling, be mindful of all scents, even those in hand lotions. I knew from personal experience how much they were attracted to floral scents and didn't wish to take the chance of arousing even honey-sedated bees.

My bee bouquet adventure had taken place in fifth grade. It was springtime and I was sitting at my desk while a bee explored the surface of my hand. While a few kids shrieked, "Look, she's letting the bee crawl on her!" I patiently waited for her to leave, and she did, flying out the window. My teacher, Mrs. Bernie, asked if I was wearing perfume and I admitted I was, something floral and secretly borrowed from my step mom's dresser that morning.

It wasn't the first time I'd been up close and personal with bees, either. At age six I discovered the fun of trapping them in baby food jars. I even got my sister Karen, who is a year younger, to join me. It was an exciting game, tracking the little creatures as they landed on dandelions and then slowly lowering the inverted jar over them, sliding the metal lid under. I'd stare at them in their little glass prison, mesmerized by the buzzing sound that came so loudly through the holes I'd punched in the top. The bees were always perturbed; it was as if they were giving me a good cussing. Nevertheless, I always enjoyed the sensation of my power over the bees, even while experiencing a definite prickle in my conscience that what I was doing wasn't really kind. We always let them go—after a little while. That particular game ended when my little sister fell and cut her hand on a glass jar (not badly, but enough for Mom to put a stop to the game).

As I prepared for the 8 A.M. call I thought about how, in the beekeeping class, we were taught to move calmly and slowly around the bees. Bees didn't have great eyesight but responded to the threat of motion near their hive. I could handle a zen-like state, the floral-free requirement, and the light clothing. People who panic easily would not be doing this anyway, I mused, envisioning the cartoon image of a person running away from a hive, a swarm of bees following in hot pursuit.

Tony called. The bees were still there, I could come right over. Driving down a picturesque road to an older subdivision sandwiched between the country club's lush green grounds and the towering white sandstone bluffs of one of our city's natural vistas, I found Tony's two-story brick colonial with the late-model truck of the second beekeeper parked out in front. Both men were standing by the truck talking. It was 8:40 A.M.

"Sorry I'm a little late," I said as I closed the car door, my camera over one shoulder and a notebook and pen in hand. "I had a hard time getting out of the house this morning—had to tend to the kids, you know."

"Oh, that's all right," said Tony. He nodded at the camera and notebook. "You'll be too busy for those, though. We thought we'd let you hold the bucket under the swarm. It's just next door, in the backyard of the house next to mine."

"Sure . . . okay." I smiled while my mind raced in regard to the magnitude of the comment—as in, this changes everything!

Tony led me to his tidy garage where he had the gear; a veil, rubber gloves, and a white jumpsuit made of paper. All ready for me to put on.

"I got this from the place that makes chips," he said, handing me the jumpsuit.

Still dazed by my change from observer to swarm-capturing participant, I wasn't quite with it mentally. My first thought was, huh? Potato chips? A second later I thought, no, you idiot, computer chips.

I took the suit and stepped into it, pulling it easily over my clothes. Yes, I thought, this could be a little Microsoft outfit. I'd never thought of the similarity in dress between beekeepers and chip makers. Then Tony handed me thick orange gloves to put on while he tied strings around my pants bottoms, making them tight against my boots and bee-entry proof.

Tony handed me the pith hat/veil combo and then helped me with the long strings of that too, carefully bringing one under each arm, crossing them in the back, then coming around to the front, tying them around my waist. The experience had a sweetness to it, as if I were a little girl being carefully dressed by her father.

Then he took a picture of me standing by his garage and I just felt silly.

"I feel a little overdressed," I said from behind the veil as I trudged through his front yard. I was a space-girl, a chipmaker, a bona fide bee-person. What about all the stuff I'd learned about the impossibility of being stung?

"No, you're fine," Tony said.

We walked to the backyard next door. Tony's partner and the homeowners, a pleasant-looking middle-aged man and his wife, stood about twenty-five feet away from the pine tree where the swarm had congregated, up on a branch about ten feet off the ground. There were two ladders set up underneath the tree, two five gallon "bee drums" (modified paint buckets with lids) and a shop vacuum. Tony's grizzled beekeeper friend looked to be wearing the same faded outfit of the evening before, along with rubber gloves and veil. I was puzzled by shop vac until the old-timer explained that he used them in swarm capturing, his own invention.

The homeowners greeted us. They were ready for the show. At some point Tony called me Marsha and I, in another dimension entirely in my bee suit, didn't notice. The atmosphere behind the veil was dark and isolating, other-worldly, adding to the surrealism of the event. I learned that the swarm came from one of Tony's two hives.

I went to the tree. There it was, the first swarm I'd ever seen, ten feet above my head. It was beautiful. There were actually two clumps, one about the size and shape of a football and one in the same shape, next to it on the branch, about one-quarter the size. Pulsating and java-colored, the bees hung amid fresh green pine needles, lively but relatively quiet. I imagined something larger, something much more menacing.

After taking a couple of pictures, I asked the neighbor lady, "Does it bother you at all that there are bee hives next door?"

"Oh no," she said. "I give them sugar water."

Her husband smiled in agreement.

The older beekeeper, whom I noticed was called Rev, walked to the tree, ready to begin. I handed my camera to Tony and followed.

* * *

Tony took my picture, then Rev handed me a bucket and lid. "I'll get the big clump with my bucket. You hold this one right under the other, and put the lid on it when the bees fall in.

We climbed the ladders and positioned ourselves. Rev gave the limb a shake.

"There they go," said someone from down below.

Many bees fell into the bucket, but hundreds didn't.

"Now they're starting to move," I heard someone say. The voice seemed far away.

Bees started flying, buzzing, covering my veil, my gloves, my clothes.

I tried to absorb all the sensations while simultaneously trying, with slow haste, to get the lid over the top of the bucket. I did, but it was upside down. I'd screwed-up and I didn't want to turn it over for fear the bees would escape. While I tried to work calmly, internally it was a non-Zen zone. I was experiencing a major adrenaline rush.

I climbed down the ladder with the bucket and confessed about the lid. Rev nonchalantly turned it over and sealed it. I looked at him through a veil blotched with bees. He was covered in them too, there were bees flying all around us, on top of the buckets, on the ladders, on the ground. How many did we get, I wondered. It seemed like a zillion still buzzed around.

We were the tamperers, in the middle of everything, and wild with the excitement of it.

Rev turned on the shop vac and began vacuuming bees off me, then I did the same for him. I told him about the bee inside his veil, near the back of his head; he said he knew. There wasn't anything either one of us could do about it anyway, not yet. It felt weird to suck up bees with a vacuum. I tried to be as gentle yet as swift as possible. My emotions were definitely mixed—I was aware that some were probably being injured, but I was also determined to do my part as a member of the homo sapien bee team.

"I'm going to vacuum the rest of the bees out of the tree," said Rev.

I looked up to see they'd returned to form several very small clumps. Rev climbed up the ladder and I held the machine while he worked. When he came down again, we repeated the process of vacuuming each other, then the containers and ladders. I saw the many bee corpses on the ground, on the ladder and on my clothes. Some were squished, but many seem to have died for no apparent reason. Their bodies looked abnormally large, full and taunt, just like they'd described. I felt very sorry for them and said so, asking how many they guessed had been killed.

"We've probably got about five thousand—what's a few here and there?" was Rev's sentiment. He was obviously excited, like me. In spite of the carnage, I shamelessly thought: This was fun! I want to do this again! I was back to age six. It was all about the rush. The rush of facing nature and claiming superiority over it. Purely animal, even more purely, human. We were the tamperers, in the middle of everything, and wild with the excitement of it.

A few bees flew around while I helped Rev pack up. He had already shed his gloves and his hat. Then I went back to the garage to take off my costume. My long hair was partially in my face, had been since I'd descended the tree the first time, and I hadn't been able to push it away. The thrill had died down by then. I had had enough of the bee suit.

By the time I dressed, Rev was gone and Tony had returned to the garage. He confirmed my suspicions that the capture was messy. "If we'd waited awhile, they would've formed one large swarm that was longer. You can usually just work your bucket right under them, practically place the whole swarm in it. And I give the branch one good hit, I don't shake it. The best way to do it is to cut the branch off and bring it straight to the hive. That way you'd probably have no deaths, but of course I couldn't do that here."

"What about the vacuuming, does it hurt them?"

"Naw, not really."

"And what's the likelihood we got the queen amid all that?"

"Oh, about 99.9%."

"Really?"

"Oh, yeah."

I asked about Rev, who had taken the bees and left.

"I just met him last night," Tony said. "I joined the Beekeepers Association about four years ago and last night was the first meeting I've been able to attend. They've always fallen on dates when I've had other engagements. By the way, Rev's a reverend."

"You're kidding!" I said. "Another surprise. I thought you two were long-time buddies."

"Nope. Never met him until last night."

I wondered at the loose communities we humans could create. Join up with some strangers who share a common interest, go out and wrangle some bees. So unlike the structured bee communities, where each stayed in their specialized tasks for a lifetime. The bees worked with the flow of nature, we seemed intent on making nature work with our flow.

Tony told me he got into beekeeping when his daughter was in junior high and they decided it would be a good science project. She soon went on to other things, namely horses, and he kept with the bees. He showed me the barrel-like, three-foot-tall, stainless-steel honey extractor in one corner of the garage that he'd bought used for five hundred dollars, explaining that even with this state-of-the-art piece of equipment it was a time-consuming project every fall, extracting and bottling his bees' work, which he gave away as gifts to his friends and neighbors.

We took a quick tour of his orderly backyard where I admired his vegetable garden with pvc bean trellises, a pond with a spouting carp fountain (Tony said the bees liked to drink from it) and, in the furthest corner, two white hives, wood boxes on stands about two feet off the ground. The hives looked so non-threatening, a working part of his garden and a positive addition to the surrounding ecosystem. As we walked up, Tony pointed out the half-dozen or so bees crawling on the landing boards near the hive entrances and said, "You see, Marsha, it's still too cool, there's very little activity right now. Later on it'll warm up and they'll start flying."

We'd been "busy bees" that morning, but in fact humans aren't anything like bees. Sure, we had cities like bees, and drove our cars and flew our planes along pre-ordained paths, much like the flight patterns of bees from their hives out to forage, but that's about where the similarities end. I wondered what type of flying insect we might best compare to. If there were a species of unusually self-centered insects, ones that believed in community but were pretty much loose and free, doing whatever the heck they wanted—well, then, we'd have our mascot.

I thanked Tony for the experience, got his phone number in case I had any more questions, and we parted.

And I never told him my name wasn't Marsha. ❀

Flower & Garden

The Creature Feature by David Rudin

Insecta 1 by Dianne Kornberg

Consider the Beetle

Ladies and gentlemen, may I present the unsung beetle. We share the planet with over 400,000 species of beetles. (For perspective, there are only 50,000 animals with backbones: fish, amphibians, reptiles, birds and mammals combined.) In fact, according to Berkeley entomologist Jerry Powell, beetles make up "almost 25% of all known life-forms." How many kinds of beetles are there yet to be discovered? Scientific guess-timates range into the millions. Beetles have managed this remarkable feat with a winning design and a flair for adaptation.

If there is a food source out there, there is a beetle adapted to exploit it. Entomologist Eric Grissell, author of *Insects and Gardens*, informs us, "There are cigarette beetles, carpet beetles, ship-timber beetles, sap beetles, drugstore beetles," (presumably loitering out front) "potato beetles, cucumber beetles and plant-boring beetles of all kinds." Yes, beetles infest tobacco products and even pharmaceuticals. Fortunately they are rarely parasitic, and never on humans. We indulge in a love/hate relationship with them as with most of the insect world. We love ladybugs (ladybird beetles actually) munching on garden aphids, marvel at fireflies (another misnamed beetle, sometimes called lightning bugs), and yet we rail against pine beetles devastating our forests, and against snout beetles, better known as weevils, destroying our crops. In my home state, the Colorado Potato Beetle is hardly a source of pride. It has spread throughout the US, Europe and now Asia, dragging the state's name through the mud as it goes. However, from a strictly scientific perspective, we might celebrate all beetles, even Colorado's state's spud-eating namesake. We have thrown every toxin known to man, including DDT, at the potato beetle and it has developed a resistance to them all. Surely, perseverance should be worth something. This ability to adapt has allowed beetles to fit into every niche imaginable and some we'd rather not imagine. We are indeed fortunate to have a wide variety of beetles evolved to eat carrion and dung. It would be disastrous if they ever went on strike or found career coaches who steered them toward more elegant occupations.

Many varieties have even conquered freshwater. The familiar Whirligig Beetles amuse us with their seemingly confused circling on a pond's surface, while a host of predacious diving beetles make their living hunting under the water's surface. The largest of these, at just an inch or two, regularly eat small fish and frogs. Ranging from the size of a pin-head to huge, cumbersome beasts over seven inches, the beetles' structure is the basically the same. What distinguishes beetles from other insects are their wings. They have hard wing covers known as elytra that meet down the middle of the body and membranous hindwings that do the flying. That basic design has been tweaked into a vast and often fabulously colorful number of varieties. Metallic greens, golds and iridescent rainbows appear like living gems and in fact have been used as such. Yet the ancient Egyptians are famous for revering an unremarkable, black dung beetle known as a scarab (from the family *Scarabaeidae*).

The scarab rolls its ball of dung along just as the Egyptian god Khepri rolled out the sun each day. In the case of the dung beetle it then buries the dung ball, laying an egg inside, thus continuing an amazing life cycle. That egg turns into a larva (commonly called a grub) then pupae and finally an adult. Even in metamorphosis, beetles offer surprises. The California Prionus Beetle spends several years underground as a grub, boring into plant roots and eating sapwood. By contrast, it spends only a few weeks as the large black adult beetle (sometimes over two inches in length) seen flying about during summer. Perhaps we should consider them grubs that go through a beetle phase, rather than the other way around.

One can find the unexpected even among the fireflies, those harbingers of warm summer evenings. They are not all sweetness and light. Different species of firefly use

Dung Beetles

different patterns when flashing their lights. These bioluminescent chemical reactions in their abdomen help males and females find one another. However, there is often an impostor lurking during these lovely summer scenes. Some fireflies have learned to mimic the flashing signals of other firefly species, thus luring them in with an invitation to mate. These impostors' true intentions are far more sinister. Their objective is to lure these other species in and then eat them.

So what then is a gardener to do? For over 300 million years beetles have evolved into their current myriad of shapes, sizes and lifestyles. These unassuming insects are found in every part of our gardens. Their complexity is so stunning as to defy any simple solution for beetle pests. My approach is to try to create a full and complex ecosystem surrounding my gardens and let the natural world sort out some type of balance. Since toxins have proven ineffective, when I feel I must meddle, I do so by simply plucking off and destroying the offending invaders. More often I enjoy seeing their amazing diversity and count their nibblings as a small fee to pay for an amazing show.

Clearly the beetle deserves our appreciation; they are in fact one of Darwin's superstars of evolution. Perhaps no group of animals has been so successful and yet remained largely unknown. As the resurgent VW Beetle has shown, we humans are suckers for a winning design. ❁

Wild with the Weeds
by Lois Hayna

We mark time, peering through
fences where luckier plants
revel in food, water and tillage.
From inhospitable edge, we
mark time. We envy their riches,
ache for their extravagance and make no
answer when they say we have
neither the genes nor the right
to their easy destiny.
Spindling, malnourished,
we bear early seed. Strong,
mobile seed. Our hopes lock on
our seed and its next generation.
Across forbidden fences,
our kind will slyly
infiltrate, to share
that wealth. We mark time.

Rachael Davis

Looking for a few Green Men and Women.

(Because at Greenwoman Magazine we're on a mission!)

We created this magazine because we want to turn people on to art, to gardening, to saving Mother Earth, stuff like that. We think that those who are connected to these things can't help but live lives that contribute to a better planet.

If you'd like to help spread the word about our publication, we'd love to send you some back issues of Greenwoman (our earlier, recycled paper version) to share with your friends. Maybe at work, school, your garden club, community garden, book group, a Meetup group. . . there are so many possibilities!

Send us a note at sandra@greenwomanmagazine.com and let's get together to make the world a little greener. Thank you!

Logo design by Mike Beenenga

Tuscan Roots by Cynthia Rosi

Armed with a machete, an ancient digging stick and a mailbag, we set out one chilly April morning to dig Tuscan roots.

My husband and I had picked up our zia (aunt) from her stone house in a village built along an Apennine spur in Lunigiana—the Valley of the Moon. Wearing Wellington boots with nylon stockings, a black skirt, and a wool-knitted vest, Zia dressed in the same style as village women in photos from World War II.

We searched for madder today, Rubia peregrina, used for thousands of years in Lunigiana to dye eggs for Holy Week and wool the bright red of a Medici cloak.

Morning dew swamped our tennis shoes as we climbed past blackberry thorns. Zia marched along and tutted at the overgrowth. "Twenty years ago there were sheep here, and potatoes," she pointed out. "Youngsters don't make money from sheep, and there are plenty vegetables in town."

Suddenly Zia stopped. She crouched next to a tree, and began to whack at the earth with her digger, an ancient-looking tool with a leather wrapped, adze-shaped head. She wormed her fingers into the rich soil and carefully followed a cord back to the mother plant. Sitting on her heels in her black skirt, our white-haired Zia grinned, "How long, do you think, have people been digging these?"

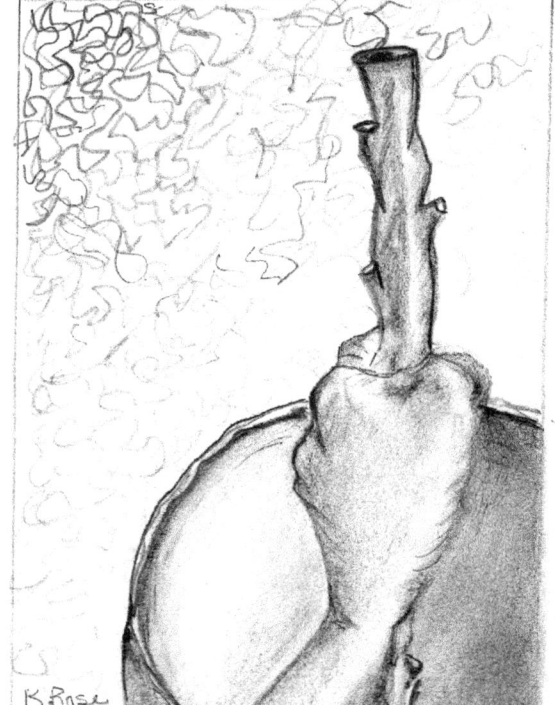

After gathering the stringy rhizomes, Zia made a bundle in her hand, and wrapped a long piece several times around the middle to tie it. Eying a broom plant, she handed my husband the machete. "For the rabbits," she explained.

As I watched him whack at the stalks, I thought of the cart-load of forage stored in Zia's outbuilding: a free source of feed for the meat.

Back at the village, we squatted in front of our Zia's stone house. We sorted and cut the madder into two-inch lengths. Zia peeled back the bark with her fingernails to show me the orangey core. "We dyed our socks red with these roots during the War," she said. I'd felt amazement at such fresh wartime memories when I came to the village from Seattle twenty years ago. During that visit

Kathleen Lindemann

my father-in-law recalled the first American he'd ever met, an African-American zooming up the road in a Willis jeep, asking which way the retreating German army went.

When the plants layered the bottom of a battered steel pot, we picked it up and turned our backs on a stunning view of the gardens: olives, vines, and snow-hooded mountains. At the village fountain, we rinsed the dusty roots under a brass spigot, scrubbed them against the pot, and dumped them all out onto the flags, only to put them back in the pot to rinse them again.

Our Zia had no problem crouching on her heels, bent double over her little chore. Her spine is perfectly straight after a lifetime of tending sheep, goats, chickens and rabbits, maintaining her garden, hunting porcini mushrooms on the mountain with her walking stick, and preparing endless plates of home-made ravioli, polenta and loaves of foccacia.

As we worked, she told me that eggs dyed with madder will be edible even if the shells break. We returned to the kitchen and the brown wood stove that is central to her home's warmth. She stoked the fire and pulled out iron rings until the bottom of the pot fit snugly into the hole, over the flame. The cut Rubia peregrina would simmer in water all day.

That evening, after adding freshly-gathered eggs to the red-black dye, I collected my son from his grandparents and took him to the end of the village. It was 7:30 p.m. and the mountains blushed pink to our left. Soon they would be silhouetted in twilight as the moon rose. The day before, we had met a cousin at market in the castle town of Pontremoli and she had invited us to visit.

When our cousin opened the door and introduced her son to my son, I saw the family resemblance in the shapes of their faces and eyes, and in their stocky builds. This is what it meant to go back to your roots.

"We're third cousins," another woman had said when introducing herself to me two years ago. Yes, I could tell. She shared my children's noses.

The eggs emerged from their bath a deep red, the color of wet jasper, almost the color of rust. We cooled them in the pot by putting it on the tile floor. The dog came to sniff and Zia fed him leftover *torta di riso*. Here dogs eat pasta, feast on minestrone and fresh chicken eggs, but this one did not like the scent of that maroon soup.

"Bring your socks tomorrow and we'll dip them in the pot," said our Zia.

We smiled, thinking of red socks to wear on our feet, warming our roots. ❋

Illustration from thegraphicsfairy.com

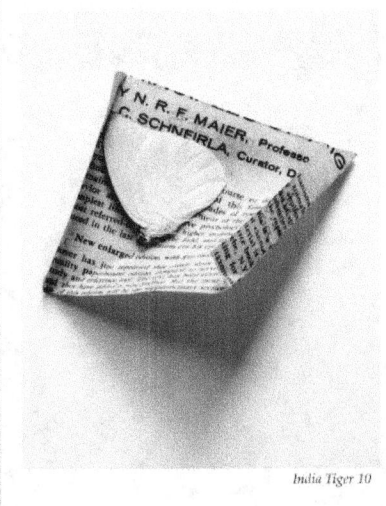

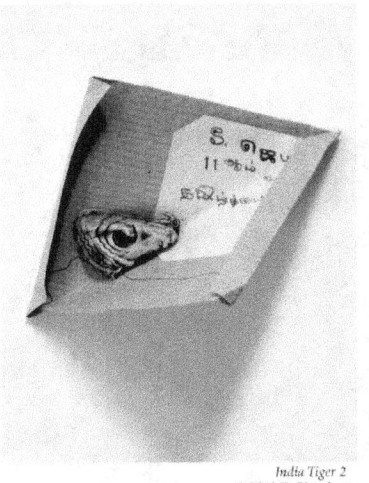
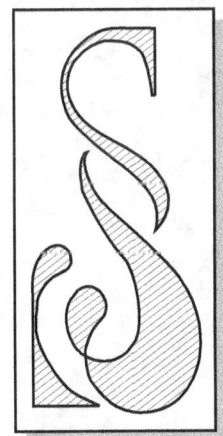

George Washington Carver:
Grandfather of Sustainability

by Cheri Colburn

Library of Congress

For weeks now I've been asking my (mostly white, mostly well-educated) friends what they know about George Washington Carver. Nearly every response has focused on the phrase, "The Peanut Guy." As you probably know, my friends are right. If there is one thing you can say about George Washington Carver, it is that he is The Peanut Guy. In fact, in his 45-year tenure at Tuskegee Institute, he single-handedly came up with well over 200 uses for the peanut. But George Carver was much more than The Peanut Guy. With a curious mix of nature, nurture, and old-fashioned good luck, he was not only an exceptional scientist and teacher; he was an exceptional human being.

Before We Begin, a Note on the Main Sources

Before I tell you just how exceptional, I feel I must offer a caveat. Throughout this article, it is not my intention to soften the effects of slavery (of course!) or racism. However, I will be offering perspectives based on my readings about George Washington Carver. One of the biographies I read— *George Washington Carver: An American Biography* by Rackham Holt—was written near the end of Carver's life and published (1944) shortly after his death. This book is a beautiful, often poetic, account, and I cannot recommend it highly enough (especially for fans of biography/memoir, fans of history, fans of gardening/agriculture, and fans of humanity).

The second book I read—*George Washington Carver: The Man Who Overcame* by Lawrence Elliot (1966)—was somewhat less compelling. (I went into the book knowing it would not so much offer Carver's own reflections but rather a more removed, objective perspective.) But by the time I read it, I was a huge Carver fan, and I wanted to know all I could find out.

The contrasts between the authorized version (herein referred to as "Holt") and this version ("Elliot"), were telling. Just a taste of this contrast is revealed by a comparison of the two subtitles: Holt's "An American Biography" reflects Carvers humility and down-to-earth perspective on his life and his work. Elliot's "The Man Who Overcame" reflects a bit more grandiosity—warranted in my opinion, but not something that (I believe) Carver would embrace.

Now, on to the story . . .

As Luck Would Have It

Carver's life began with a sizeable portion of bad luck. He was born in 1861 (some more recent accounts say 1864) near Diamond Grove (now Diamond), Missouri in a slave cabin owned by Moses Carver and his wife Sue. From the start, he was a weak and sickly baby, and (insult to injury) when he was still virtually a newborn, he and his mother were stolen by night raiders during the Missouri/Kansas border wars. Moses Carver sent a man to find them, and that man returned with only baby George, near death, wrapped in rawhide. Perhaps his mother, "Carver's Mary" died from rough treatment so early after giving birth to baby George, or perhaps she was simply sold away, but the sad fact is that his mother was gone from him forever. Because his father had died on a neighboring plantation before his birth, Carver was an orphan from the start.

Moses Carver had a fairly small operation—basically a subsistence farm—but he still needed help to run it, and that help came from slaves. Moses owned George's mother, Mary (and her children), and for a time he had owned George's father. But Moses was never in full support of slavery, and he was apparently glad when it ended. (Both biographies assert that he sent the scout to find Mary and George not to reclaim his property, but out of concern for their well-being.) Sue and Moses were both greatly pleased when sick baby George was returned to them.

According to my sources, two years after Carver's birth the Emancipation Proclamation was signed, but little changed in young George's life or in the life of his brother, Jim. Moses and Sue Carver raised both boys as if they were their own children. The Carvers were well-respected people (even though, in a community of Christians, they did not attend church), and they took excellent care of the boys as they grew. George, who never became particularly strong, stayed in the house with "Aunt Sue," where he learned several homemaking skills—sewing, cooking, and the like—that would serve him throughout his life.

"I Want to Know"

Far from shunning household labor as "women's work," young George cherished his growing skills and knowledge. In fact, while still a child, George was heard to say that when he grew up, he would start a school to teach other boys how make a home.

He was also known for asking "Why?" Consider this quote from Holt: "A huge insatiable question mark had been in his mind ever since he could think at all: 'I want to know.' He fed it fuel constantly, and it was never satisfied. But it did repay him with energy; his 'I want to know,' followed by its corollary, 'I can do that,' was the dynamo that powered his life."

Moses and Sue Carver did their best to help George satisfy his appetite for learning. In addition to practical skills, Sue Carver (virtually illiterate herself) taught George every word in her copy of Webster's "blue-back speller," and George was allowed to attend Sunday School where he began to learn to read.

Unlike many black children of his era, George Carver had a real childhood. When he was just a little boy, he was allowed to wander through the woods, where he had a little plant hospital; neighbors and friends would give him ailing plants, and he would take them into the woods and nurse them back to health. George never lost a patient and came to be known as "the plant doctor."

Once he was invited to the home of a neighbor to help some failing rose bushes. That day changed the direction of George Carver's life forever. After moving the roses from the shade into the sun, George was invited inside. On the walls of that parlor hung several paintings—the first George had ever seen. He was mesmerized. His "I can do that" spirit kicked in, and from that day forward, he made pictures with whatever he could find. He began by scratching images onto wood with coal and nails, and throughout his life, he drew and painted whenever and wherever he could. Indeed, he seemed unable not to paint. Making art became central to who he was as a human being, and his love for making art provided a counterpoint to his career as a scientist.

Ten Years Old and On His Own: Neosho and "Aunt Mariah"

Carver's appetite for knowledge drove him (always) toward school. He could not attend the school in Diamond Grove because it was only for white children. (Separatism and racism were sad specters in Carvers life and times, but I believe it is a testament to his character that he would not allow their wounds to deter him from his own sense of right and wrong or from his own drive toward excellence. But I digress.) Jim and George often ran errands for Uncle Moses in the nearby town of Neosho. On one such trip, George saw a school for black children. When he arrived home, he told Moses and Sue what he

had seen and begged to attend the school. But he needn't have begged at all. Moses told George that he was free and could follow his heart's desire.

Tears stood in Moses' and Sue's eyes the day they sent 10-year-old George down the road with his little pack of food, his cherished pocket knife, and not much else. George did not even know where he would sleep that night: Nobody in Neosho was expecting him. (Can you imagine? He was just a boy!) But Carver had a knack for finding good people. After spending the first night in a hayloft, he awoke, hungry, and headed for the school.

> "George never lost a patient and came to be known as 'the plant doctor.' "

The school had not yet opened when he arrived, and George perched on a woodpile near a neighboring home. That is where Mariah Watkins found him. Mariah and her husband Andy were well-respected members of the local black community, where they attended church and where Mariah worked as a midwife and laundress. (In fact, Mariah delivered both black and white babies and was widely and deeply loved by people of both races.) Again George was treated as a member of the family, and again he learned many fine skills that would serve him throughout his life.

Compared with the Carvers, Mariah and Andy Watkins had a bit higher standard of living. They did not have a lot of money, but they had a beautiful home that they worked hard to maintain. Here, George learned about the comfort and self-respect that a beautiful home can provide. He learned home maintenance skills, such as how to whitewash walls and sand floors, and he polished what he already knew about the importance of order and discipline. Working alongside Aunt Mariah to clean customer's clothing, George refined his ironing and laundry skills (often scrubbing clothes with a book propped in front of him).

Aunt Mariah also helped George improve his sewing skills, including fine stitching and embroidery. He always loved working with his hands, and these finer skills inspired him. During this time, he saw a fancy lace collar on a white woman in town. In stolen, private moments, he copied the fine lacework and presented a copy of the collar as a Christmas gift to an astonished Aunt Mariah. Lace-making became Carver's lifelong hobby; his hands were rarely idle.

Carver also received a spiritual education while

living with Aunt Mariah. The same Christmas he presented her with a lace collar, Aunt Mariah gave George a Bible, which Carver read every day for the rest of his life, marking his place with his first effort at embroidery. George also attended church with Aunt Mariah and Uncle Andy, who were devout Christians.

Of course he attended school as well. The first day that George climbed over the fence that separated the Watkins house from the schoolyard, Aunt Mariah reminded him that he was free. No longer was he "Carver's George." In keeping with the custom of the times, he became George Carver.

The schoolhouse was a tiny 11' x 14' cabin. Each morning 75 pupils stuffed themselves into the room so tightly that when one person in a row moved, everybody had to make adjustments. The walls were thin, and the children were alternatively freezing or roasting, but few complained. They were there for a higher purpose—to learn.

The man charged with teaching them was Stephen Frost, a rather small-minded (if literate) man who tried to school his pupils in more than just the three "Rs." Luckily, George Carver had the wherewithal to resist Stephen Frost's indoctrination; otherwise, a great historical figure might have remained a kitchen hand for life. Elliot's book describes Stephen Frost and Carver's contact with him:

"'Know your place!' the teacher admonished repeatedly, imbuing the class with his own servility and a sharply limited horizon. And instinctively, silently, George rebelled. He did not delude himself: the color of his skin was a shackle. But he would shake it off or, if he must, drag it behind, for his place was in the sun, and he yearned to climb as near to it as energy and enterprise would take him."

When Carver reached his teens, he had come as close to that metaphorical sun as Stephen Frost could bring him. In addition, he had begun to think that perhaps a different climate might help him shake his sickly tendencies. So when Aunt Mariah told George that the Smith family was willing to give him a ride the 75 miles to the town of Fort Scott, George left Neosho and his happy home.

Self-Sufficiency, Racism, and Carver's Quest for Education

The Smith family dropped George off on Main Street and drove away. Once again he was in a strange town with nobody expecting him. He needed work and a place to stay. He began knocking on kitchen doors and was directed toward the home of Lucy Payne, who needed help cooking for her very particular husband. George assured her he was up to the task, but that was a bit of an overstatement. George was used to cooking very basic foods, and Mr. Payne was used to eating a more refined diet. George was in a tight spot. He told Miss Lucy that he would like to watch how she prepared the food so that he would do it just right. George's habit of "I want to know" and "I can do that" served him once again: Mr. Payne congratulated his wife on finding such a fine cook.

George Washing Carver, circa 1870s.

After George had saved enough money for books and a place to stay (he had been living in a small room under the Payne's back stairs), he left his position and went to school. That became the rhythm of his life for the next two years. He worked until he had money to go to school. Then he went to school until the money ran out. During this time, George did all kinds of household work, making the most of both his skills and his work ethic.

But none of George's hard work, none of his good luck, and none of his native talent and studious nature could protect him from the racism that was all around him. His authorized biography (Holt) mentions very few racist incidents, reflecting Carver's tendency to stay on his own path regardless of racism and ignorance (and emphasizing the impact on Carver of racists experiences that are mentioned). The story I'm about to tell is not mentioned in Holt at all.

One day Carver (who was in his middle teens) was walking down a street in Fort Scott, carrying his schoolbooks and enjoying the day, when two white men stopped him. They asked him where he got the books, and they demanded that he give the books to them. When George refused, asserting that he had bought them and they were his books, the men—in broad daylight and in front of many very silent witnesses—beat him to the ground and took his books. (Imagine such a trauma for a motherless teenager alone in the world!) George had no money to buy new books, so he simply picked himself up and began looking for work again.

He found the work he needed in the home of a blacksmith. One night during his tenure in that position, he came upon a horrifying and brutal scene. George was returning from a few errands when, from a hiding spot deep in a shadow, he watched an angry white mob pull a black man from the jail, beat him to death in the street, and set his remains on fire in the public square. From Holt: "[George] shuddered through the night, and before daylight could reveal the scene of man's ferocity he was away out of that place forever."

Closer to the Sun—
and The Great Eclipse

Thus began ten years of working and schooling. Carver met and worked for many fine people. He continued his hobbies of lace-making, gardening, reading, and when he had supplies, painting. For work, he "cooked, scrubbed clothes, chopped wood, tended gardens, cleaned rugs, dug ditches, picked fruit, hammered nails, swabbed out-houses, whitewashed fences—whatever anyone wanted done" (Elliot). Over and over again, his "I can do that!" spirit came through. Carver grew into an honorable and God-fearing man, never taking charity but always willing to help people in need. He also developed what would become a lifelong habit of walking at dawn—trudging through whatever natural space was available and bringing home bits of interest such as rocks, Native American artifacts, and plants he wished to investigate.

At one point, Carver lived in a town that had another George Carver. When Carver realized that his mail was often delivered to the wrong George Carver, he decided to take a middle initial. People often asked what the "W" stood for, repeatedly suggesting that it stood for Washington. At some point, Carver (who was not altogether comfortable with what might be perceived as the grandiosity of the name) quit correcting people. He became George Washington Carver.

When Carver was in his early 20s and enrolled in his final year of high school, he received a sad letter from Aunt Mariah. Nearly a year before, his brother Jim, al-

ways much heartier than George, had died from smallpox. Carver felt severed from his childhood and driven toward the bright light of higher education. He wanted to attend college.

Carver began sending out applications and was eventually accepted to Highland College in Highland, Kansas. Quickly he put his affairs in order and took a "nostalgic tour," visiting Uncle Moses and Aunt Sue (now in their 70s), Uncle Andy and Aunt Mariah, and Jim's grave. Finally, in September, he presented himself to the principal of Highland College. From Holt:

"The principal was busy and looked up sharply from his desk. 'Well, what do you want?'

'I am George W. Carver, sir. I've come to matriculate.'

'We take only Indians here, no Negroes.'"

That was the full extent of the conversation. The principal of the school had barely glanced at Carver before dousing his bright dream. With no money and no destination, Carver wandered to the train station where he sat long into the night. He wanted desperately to leave the scene of his devastation, but he had no choice but to find work.

Once again, he wandered, taking whatever work he could find. But this time things were different. His dream was dead. He believed now that his path was merely to make the best of his circumstances. Again, he found work where he could. He worked in a greenhouse and was fired by the nasty, racist owner who accused him of stealing. He thought he might start a greenhouse of his own, but he did not have the resources.

Carver eventually landed in the Beeler household. The Beelers had a son who was homesteading and in 1886, casting about for some hope, Carver filed his own 160-acre claim south of Beeler Kansas. He built a sod house and put in crops.

George had to work while waiting for his crops to grow. For awhile, he worked for a family of racists; they are not necessarily worthy of a place in history, so I won't dwell except to quote (from Holt) Carver's considerable insight into the matter of racism:

"He warned himself that when he had hateful thoughts about Mrs. Steeley, he was ruining his disposition and becoming just as hateful as she. He urged that at heart she was a good person, but was afflicted with a feeling of being inferior, which forced her to dominate somebody or other to try to prove she was superior."

And so George Carver was to live his whole life. All through his years at Tuskegee (which I will get to in a moment), he rarely gave racists a bit of his concern. He just kept moving forward, focused on his own purpose.

Carver's Place in the Sun

In 1890 or thereabouts, Carver met the (white) Milholland family at the Methodist Church where he attended services. When Mrs. Milholland heard George sing, she wanted to know him better. (Carver had a beautiful tenor voice, and his "I want to know" spirit had driven him to learn to use it and to play a little music.) The family invited George into their home, and he and Mrs. Milholland discovered they had much in common. Mrs. Milholland had a greenhouse and, like Carver, a passion for gardening. She was also an amateur painter. When George saw the sorry condition of her brushes and palette, he immediately began to set them right. Seeing that he was expert with the tools, Mrs. Milholland asked if he had advice for the painting she had underway. From that point forward, Carver gave her painting instruction in exchange for piano lessons.

Over time Carver became great friends with the Milhollands, and their home was often his as well. As they got to know Carver better, the Milhollands began to appreciate that he was a serious student. (Carver had set up a school for himself and kept strict hours for each subject.) Whether Carver would allow himself to hope for it or not, the Milhollands knew he should go to college.

They also knew that Simpson College in Iowa had been endowed by Matthew Simpson, a Methodist bishop and friend of Abraham Lincoln. Simpson had been a believer in the equality of all men, and Mr. Milholland assured Carver that Simpson College would accept him if only he would go. But—after Carver's disappointment at Highland years before—he required persistent persuasion. Eventually they won him over. One day while scrubbing a customer's clothes in his little home/laundry service, Carver's light came back on. He would go to college.

Carver, now nearly 30 years old, entered Simpson in the fall of 1890, enrolling in all the classes you'd expect (along with a preparatory course in math, his weak point). Then he presented himself to the art teacher, Miss Etta Budd. She was shocked that a black student would want to enter such an impractical course and required that Carver prove himself and his skills. After two weeks of restless anxiety and labored sketching, Carver did just that. He went on to become one of the finest students Miss Budd had ever known.

A friendship grew between Carver and Miss Budd, and so did her concern for his welfare. Although he was a talented student, she knew of no black people who made a living with art. She spoke with him about the possibility of pursuing a more practical path.

In fact, Carver had been very happy at Simpson, where he was finally free to paint to his heart's content and where he had formed many satisfying friendships. But Carver had been troubled by a sense that he should be doing more to help his people. Aunt Mariah's words, uttered when Carver was just a boy, rang in his ears—"Go out in the world and give your learning back to our people. They're starving for a little learning."

So when Miss Budd told Carver that she had spoken with her father— J.L. Budd, Professor of Horticulture at Iowa Agricultural College in Ames— and that Ames would take him, Carver sadly agreed that he should go. He enrolled at Ames in May of 1891.

During his time at Ames—both as a student and later as an instructor—Carver studied mycology extensively. (I will save you the time I spent looking up *mycology*: it is the study of fungi.) His descriptions and discoveries of several fungi were added to the general library on the subject. In fact, several fungi are named for Carver; just watch for *carveri* in your mycological meanderings, and you will find a testament to his work.

Carver's achievements and hard work found a counter-balance in his general enjoyment of life. He joined clubs. He played music at school and community events. He attended church. He made countless friends and was admired by people who knew him. He created an unknown number paintings (unknown because many of them were destroyed in a fire at Tuskegee in the years following his death), and his talent was widely recognized.

In fact, during his Ames years, some classmates

entered one of his paintings for consideration by the organizers of the Worlds Columbian Exposition (aka, "The World's Fair") in Chicago. "Yucca and Cactus" was accepted for show. As you might suspect, plants were frequently the subject of Carver's painting; they were a beautiful combination of his love for art, his love for the natural world, and his interest (conceived in his "plant hospital") in the why and how of plant forms and habits.

In 1896, Carver received his Master's Degree in agriculture and bacterial botany and began teaching at Ames. He was content but had dis-ease with that contentment, an ongoing nagging belief that he should be doing more to help his race. Then, in April of 1896, he received a letter from the African American leader, Booker T. Washington:

> *I cannot offer you money, position, or fame. The first two you have. The last, from the place you now occupy, you will no doubt achieve. These things I now ask you to give up. I offer you in their place work—hard, hard work—the task of bringing a people from degradation, poverty and waste to full manhood. (Elliot)*

Washington was offering Carver the opportunity to head the agricultural department at Tuskegee, a struggling and impoverished black college in Alabama. And in that offer, according to Elliot, "God had revealed His plan for George Carver."

In Service to His Race

As the train jostled from Ames, Iowa, to Tuskegee, Alabama, in October of 1896, George Washington Carver, now 35, contemplated the people he saw working in the country-side. It was harvest season, and every available hand was in the cotton fields. As the train passed, African American men, women, and children would straighten a bit, look with flat expression toward the train and then bend again into their work. Already Carver was getting a sense of slavery's aftermath in the Deep South.

George Washington Carver (front and center) with staff members at the Tuskegee Institute. (Library of Congress)

Carver likely also contemplated the task he had agreed to undertake. He had myriad responsibilities at Tuskegee. Perhaps most obviously, he was to teach. He was also charged with making money for Tuskegee's operating expenses by planting cash crops. Last and most importantly, he was to contribute his efforts to the over-riding goal of the school: to educate and improve the lives of African Americans. Carver held this final goal most closely.

Carver the Teacher

Farming had a tarnished reputation in the South, and many of the students who came to Tuskegee wanted to study other things. Carver knew, however, that most of his students were destined to return to the family farm. He persuaded students to enter the School of Agriculture by selling it as "agricultural science" instead of "farming."

Nevertheless, once enrolled, his students found themselves engaged in harshly familiar work. They tilled the soil, cleared land, and planted crops. But they also received a whole new perspective on the study of plants and how they grow. In fact, this perspective was not just new to his students: It was new to the field of botany.

Carver had long been frustrated by traditional teaching methods, which he perceived focused on erudite and impractical information geared toward scientists rather than useful application. From Holt: "The object was to know plants, or why study it? Instead the student was given a lot of technical terms, and when he had learned those he did not really know plants." Carver proposed that plants be taught in like groups and that as each plant or type of plant was learned, its diseases be presented as well. He put plants "into the great family by common characteristics and subdivided into the smaller groups by distinct differences."

In addition to teaching agriculture, botany, and

related subjects, Carver held Bible study classes. He was somewhat nontraditional both in his manner of presenting information (often theatrically) and in his beliefs. According to Holt, Carver once said, "Nothing is more beautiful than the loveliness of the woods before sunrise. At no other time have I so sharp an understanding of what God means to do with me as in these hours of dawn. When other folk are still asleep, I hear God best and learn his plan."

Holt wrote further of Carver's Sunday morning talks: "For Professor Carver no conflict existed between religion and science; science confirmed the Scriptures rather than opposed them, and God and the spiritual world were closely united to the natural world." Later in his life, Carver was the object of some suspicion for his poorly understood and often misquoted religious views, but he held fast. As far as he was concerned, God was to be found not only in church but also in the very dirt beneath our feet.

Carver the Scientist

With this subject—dirt—Carver was deeply concerned. After all, he was charged with making money via crops to help support the mission of Tuskegee.

Tuskegee had some benefactors, but the goal was to be self-supporting, and in this effort, student tuition was not much help. Students were never turned away from Tuskegee, and many of them worked their way through. They worked in the fields, baked bricks from clay soil, built badly needed new structures, dug ditches to route water. They cooked, they cleaned, they sewed, and they did laundry. But they often did not pay tuition.

As a result, the school badly needed to show a profit in the form of crops, and mak-

Peanut

ing money from the land surrounding Tuskegee was no small task. Like most of the land in the South, Tuskegee's grounds had been completely wasted by cotton—a deep feeder that had blanketed the land for over a century. Carver knew that the soil must be enriched, and he implemented new practices to do so. While established practice said that plowing should be shallow, he plowed deep so that the plants could reach fertile soil. While established practice said that last year's growth should be burned off, Carver tilled dead stalks back into the ground. While established practice said that kitchen waste was garbage, he mined garbage heaps for their rich soil, tilling it back into the fields. He also began a compost pit, adding all of the school's organic waste—paper, leaves, rags, grass, weeds, kitchen waste, street sweeping—anything that would rot.

Over time, Tuskegee began to make money from the land. "The loss from the Station the first year was $2.50 an acre. The next year also the ledger read $2.50, but in black instead of red. In seven years, with no commercial fertilizer whatever, it profited $75 an acre." (Holt)

New Crops and New Products

One of the ways that Carver increased the yield (and the profit) at Tuskegee was to diversify the crops. Among the crops he planted were legumes—chiefly cowpeas and peanuts. (He also experimented with a new crop from Asia, which we now know as the ubiquitous soybean). Carver knew that legumes add nitrogen to the soil, and he knew that Southern soils were in desperate need of this vital nutrient. For similar reasons, he also encouraged the planting of sweet potatoes. (Sweet potatoes, a member of the morning glory family by the way, do not actually add nitrogen to the soil, but they don't exhaust it either.)

Carver knew that the crops he championed were good not only for the health of Southern soils but also for the health of Southern people. Carver was deeply concerned with what he observed to be an unhealthy diet of cheap meat and starch purchased in the stores of white landholders. He knew that if Southern black farmers diversified their plantings, both their health and their wallets would be improved.

Cowpeas (better known, by me at least, as black-eyed peas) had long been grown as livestock feed, but Carver encouraged people to add them to their own diets. He also knew that "Pound for pound the peanut topped sirloin for proteins, the best potatoes for carbohydrates, and the best butter for fat." (Holt) And he knew, as most nutrition-conscious people today know, that sweet potatoes are extremely high in vitamin A and fairly high in vitamin C as well (not to mention high-quality, fiber-rich carbohydrate).

But there was a double-edged problem. First, people must be convinced that these crops were both nutritious and delicious. Second, they needed to be able to make money on what they planted. In other words, if the Southern farmer was going to plant legumes and sweet potatoes, there needed to be commercial demand. Carver set to work.

Carver knew that the crops he recommended would have to be not only pleasing to the soils, but pleasing to the palate as well. Most families had always planted a few "goobers" here and there next to fence posts as treats for their children and sometimes as feed for livestock. Carver wanted to convince them that legumes could be a larger part of their diets, so he used the cooking skills he'd developed over decades to create over 100 ways to prepare peanuts for consumption—including dishes as wide-ranging as mock chicken and desserts. He also created 18 recipes using the cowpea.

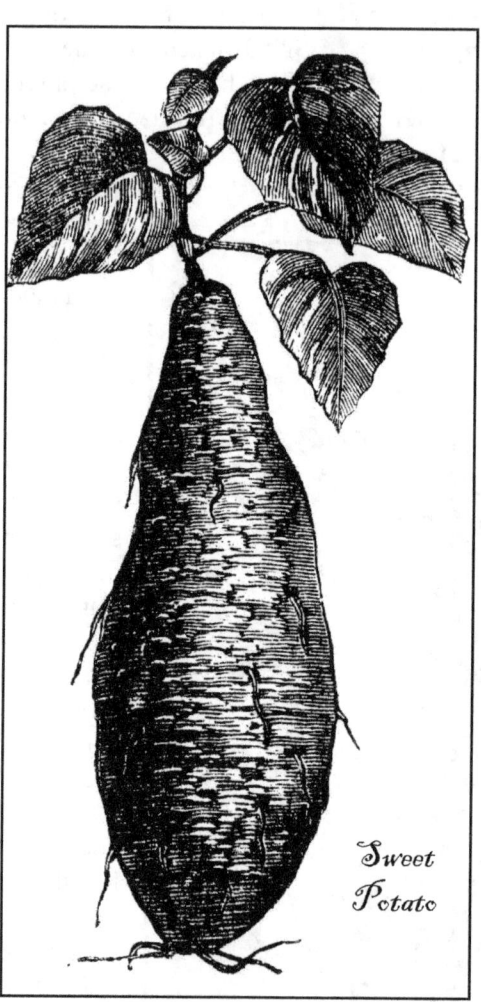

Sweet Potato

Still, Carver knew farmers were in business to make money. He needed to create a commercial demand for these crops, and toward this end, he worked tirelessly. Carver built a laboratory wholly created with materials salvaged from the garbage heap. (Carver and his students punched holes in tin to make graders, found reeds to use as makeshift pipettes, and reclaimed a cracked china bowl for use as a mortar.) In this lab, Carver broke plants down into their component parts to discover industrial applications. He called this study "synthetics," and he was quite successful. (It's ironic, really, that the word *synthetic* used to have such a progressive feel to it; now it is virtually synonymous with *fake*.)

In his lab, Carver created hundreds of products from the peanut. He created (merely for example) milk, butter, meal, cold drinks, oil (cooking, salad, and industrial), lotions, face creams, and face powder. From the sweet potato, he created laundry starch that could be made not only commercially but also at home (theoretically improving the bearing of all those who used it).

Carver not only created new products; he also worked to stimulate a demand for them. In this last effort—stimulating demand—Carver was helped along by the first World War, which brought the flow of German chemicals, fertilizers, and dyes to an abrupt halt. The head of one dye producer, upon learning of Carver's work, sent him a blank check indicating that Carver could come to work for his company and become a wealthy man. Carver declined that offer and many similar offers over the years (including a $100,000-per-year offer from Thomas Edison, which would be over $1 million dollars today). In fact, Carver's wish was for enterprising people to take his ideas and develop them; he never profited from his inventions and rarely even took a patent.

Carver rarely profited financially from any of his tireless effort. He was hired at Tuskegee for a salary of $125 per month, and that was his wage for nearly 40 years until he died. Carver was hard-pressed to even find time to cash his paychecks (which confounded Tuskegee's bookkeepers). Instead, his habit was to stash them into books or boxes and to offer them up when hard-working students needed assistance or when Booker T. Washington himself told Carver of the school's need. When he died, Carver had over $30,000 in the bank, and he donated that money back to Tuskegee.

Seeds of Knowledge

Carver's mission was clear, and he had no split loyalties: He desired to improve the lives of African Americans. This, of course, was the mission of Tuskegee itself, and Booker T. Washington sought to make it the mission of Tuskegee graduates as well. During commencement exercises, Washington would say things like "Go back to the place where you came from and work. Don't waste too much time looking for a paying job. If you can't get pay, ask for the privilege of working for nothing." In that spirit, many "little Tuskegees" cropped up in small settlements and at crossroads across the south from Virginia to Texas.

But this method of spreading ideas and information was too slow for Carver's purpose. He knew that black farmers were in crisis, and he wanted to ease their suffering sooner not later. So Carver created other ways to reach the farmers. His first year at Tuskegee, he set up an Experiment Station to show what could be done to enrich the soil and improve yields. One of his first experiments was to plow the old kitchen dump and plant crops such as onions, watermelons, and corn.

This experimental garden became a showplace of productive fertility. The yield was high, and the fruit and vegetables were large. So that his results would reach the people who needed the information, he invited Southern farmers (both black and white) to visit the school. These "Demonstration Days" began small but soon grew to include hundreds of people yearning to know more.

Eventually the Demonstration Days became the Farmer's Institute. Once a month, farmers and their wives would come to Tuskegee to receive information and instruction regarding a vast array of topics. They learned about soils and new crops, of course, and they also learned about homemaking: cooking, quilt-making, home-maintenance, and gardening. Basically, they received information about living more productive, healthier—and even more beautiful—lives.

With regard to the importance of beauty, Carver had a lot to say, and his thinking was right in line with Booker T. Washington's. Washington was keenly aware that his school would be judged in large part on its appearance, and he wisely put Carver in charge of beautifying the campus. His first winter at Tuskegee, Carver began to transform the grounds. He had the land terraced, and in the spring (in addition to crops), trees, grasses, and flowers were planted.

As Tuskegee became more widely known, Northerners came to tour the campus and the surrounding farms. Booker T. Washington appealed to Southern blacks to spruce-up their properties by painting and whitewashing their homes, recommending that if they could not afford to paint the whole house to at least paint the front. This effort built on itself, and each year the properties looked better than the year before.

This effort greatly pleased Carver who felt that when one's property was improved, so was one's self-worth. There had been a notable absence of pride in the appearance of Southern black homes, largely because improving a property owned by a white landlord might increase one's rent. But the sharp contrast between Southern black homes and the homes Carver had seen

and helped to operate in the north was troubling to Carver. He encouraged people to pay more attention to this issue—to paint their homes, to plant flowers for their simple beauty, to maintain their living space (inside and out) for their own comfort and pleasure. Carver also had a sense that beauty—especially the beauty of a well-tended garden—brought one closer to God.

"As part of his effort to disseminate information, he started publishing bulletins . . . on topics such as soil conservation, crop rotation, and composting."

As time passed and farmers' successes accumulated, excitement grew. More and more people attended the Farmer's Institute and joined in the demonstrations, bringing their products for show and discussion. From this new pride grew the Macon County Fair—and soon after many other county fairs. Produce was the focus of the first fair (in 1898), but the women soon got involved, adding quilts, canned goods, needlework and home-cured meat to the displays. In 1903, Professor Carver spoke at the fair, extolling the benefits of (what else?) sweet potatoes and cowpeas.

In fact, Carver—a naturally quiet and modest man—had been a public speaker since his days at Ames. Back then, he would lecture at mycological gatherings (and of course in the classroom). But from his earliest days at Tuskegee, he spoke at small gatherings of farmers. Carver had a wagon that he drove into the countryside to reach people who could not attend Demonstration Days or the Farmers' Institute. In it, he carried information about increasing profits and improving health—along with preserves, seeds, and even slips of roses to share. During these outings, Carver would often stay in the very modest homes of the people he was seeking to help. People were proud to have such an important man staying in their homes, and Carver was such a warm and unassuming person that any intimidation they might have felt quickly dissipated. He was not only admired but widely loved.

Carver's speaking efforts and skills eventually reached a broad and prestigious audience. Widely known as a champion of the lowly peanut, Carver was invited one year to speak at the Peanut Growers' Association. He astounded the (white) men who were in attendance with all he had learned and all of the products he had developed. As a result of that presentation, he was invited to speak on behalf of the Peanut Growers Association in a presentation to Congress in 1921. Peanuts from China were threatening the ability of US growers to make money on their crops, and they wanted Congress to institute a tariff. Carver waited many hours for his turn to speak and was then told that he only had a few minutes. He opened his boxes, began to speak, and as always, captivated the attention of his audience. He was allowed to deliver his entire message, and in the end, the peanut growers got their tariff.

Carver was not only a gifted speaker; he was an accomplished writer as well. As a part of his effort to disseminate information, he started publishing bulletins as soon as his work at Tuskegee began. He published the findings from the experiment station on topics such as soil conservation, crop rotation, and composting. And he published bulletins on nearly every topic that he thought would improve the lives and profits of Southern farmers: his peanut, cowpea, and sweet potato recipes; ways to preserve food; raising chickens and animal husbandry. Carver also wrote a syndicated newspaper column—"Professor Carver's Advice"—in which he answered readers' questions.

Whenever possible, Carver tried to be proactive regarding insect infestations and livestock diseases. He wanted farmers to have the information about these problems in hand before the problems arrived. And so it was with the boll weevil. When he recognized that a plague of boll weevils was advancing on Alabama, he published a bulletin advising farmers to diversify their plantings. Many farmers listened to him, creating a surplus of peanuts and sweet potatoes and inspiring his work (mentioned previously) to create commercial markets for these crops.

As if all of Carver's aforementioned accomplishments are not enough to make us all feel like a bunch of TV-watching slackers, I will tell you that this (not so) little article barely scratches the surface of Carver's contributions. He tracked the weather for the bureau in Montgomery. He continued to study fungi throughout his life and to make contributions to the general library of information on the subject. He also contributed to efforts to catalog medicinal plants for the Smithsonian Institution and the Pan-American Medical Congress. As a child in Mariah Watkin's household, he was taught to believe in the curative powers of plants. As a result of this effort, he did not merely consider plants that were well-accepted as medicinal plants; sensing that many plants had poorly understood potential, he also those considered plants known only as household remedies.

Carver found time to help not only with academic efforts but also with earthier concerns. From the beginning, farmers could bring him soils for testing and receive advice about fertilizer. They could bring weeds for naming and receive advice about control techniques. They could bring him well-water for testing and receive not only information about its potability but also the advice to install a pump: when you lower a bucket into a well, you are introducing bacteria from your hands, from the cattle you've just been tending, from the chickens who scratch in the surrounding dirt. Essentially he would help any common man who would also help himself.

A Worldwide Audience

As Carver became more and more widely known (mostly as a result of speaking before Congress) important people from around the world began to consult with him. The Colonial Secretary of the German Empire came to Tuskegee to observe Carver's cotton hybrids. A man from Queensland Australia acquired some seed from Carver and passed it to the Australian government. Carver heard back years later that the crop was being grown successfully all over the country.

African heads of state also consulted with Carver about his pet crop (the peanut of course). The peanut is a hearty plant and came to America in the hulls of slave ships. Originally from the tropics, it can withstand draught better than most plants, shriveling in the heat but coming back to life with just a hint of moisture. In addition, it seeds itself by becoming top-heavy and bending its seeds back toward the earth.

As a result of Carver's advice, peanut "milk" put an end to a tragic practice that had formerly been carried out in African nations where cattle could not be kept. When mothers died in childbirth, their infants were often buried with them. With the peanut, these children could survive.

In the mid-1930's, Carver stepped in to help save children in the US from polio. He suspected that peanut oil massaged into the skin would enter the body providing nutrients and reinvigorating wasted limbs. Indeed, he experienced some success with the method, and soon people lined with their children, hoping for "Carver's cure." He worked tirelessly for months and managed to help many children. (Since Carver's time, it has been determined that it was most likely the massage, as opposed to the curative power of the peanut, that improved limb function for victims of polio.)

Carver's Personal Life

Though Carver loved children, he never had any of his own. Once he attempted to foster a boy at Tuskegee, but the boy did not have the disposition for hard work and study, and he eventually left Carver's side. Carver never married, and although both of the books I read mention one woman who caught his eye, little came of that relationship. In Holt's version of events (which presumably matches Carver's own), she did not understand his devotion to his work; in Elliot's version, Carver would not ask her to.

Since Carver's death, there has been speculation that he did not marry because he was gay. And perhaps that was the case. I often found myself, reading about certain subtle details of his life, wondering if he might be gay. He was recently (2007) included in *An Encyclopedia of Gay, Lesbian, Bisexual, Transgender, and Queer Culture* based partly on Holt's account of his life. Specifically, Holt describes Carver's late-life devoted friendship with his assistant, Austin W. Curtis, Jr.

Indeed, Carver willed his portion of the profits from Holt's book to Curtis, and (perhaps notably), Tuskegee fired Curtis upon Carver's death.

But Carver was a private man, and he lived during a time when public figures were allowed truly private lives. In fact, failing to subscribe to the notion that his intimate life (or possibly his lack thereof) is our business, I feel I've said more than I should have. But I wondered about it, and I thought you might be wondering too, so there it is. If you want to know more on the subject, I leave you to the library stacks.

Carver's Legacy

Over time (and partly owing to his speech before Congress), Carver became a *famous* and *important* man (back then, the meaning of the words famous and important were much more closely aligned than they are today, and his efforts attracted the attention of many other famous and important people. He became close friends with Henry Ford, for example. In fact, their affection was so great that late in Carver's life, when he became frail, Ford had an elevator installed in Carver's building at Tuskegee. Further examples of Carver's famous and important visitors include the Prince of Wales, the Crown Prince of Sweden, the Vice President of the United States, and (after Booker T. Washington's funeral), the President as well.

Carver received many awards and other forms of recognition. A museum was built in his honor at Tuske-

gee; the NAACP gave him an award for outstanding achievement; he was awarded a Roosevelt medal for distinguished service in the field of science; the University of Rochester awarded him a Doctor of Science degree. This list goes on, but in deference to Carver's own disposition (and if you've made it this far, in deference to your time), I want to keep the focus on his more down-to-earth contributions, which I hope you've tasted throughout this article.

Toward the end of 1942, Carver fell down a flight of stairs and never fully recovered, eventually taking to bed. On January 5, 1943, his friend and Tuskegee's cooking teacher brought him a tray of food from which Carver accepted only a few sips of milk and spoke his last words, "I think I will rest now." And so he did.

Carver's epitaph reads: "He could have added fortune to fame, but caring for neither, he found happiness and honor in being helpful to the world."

What an amazing man. ✻

Illustration from the U. S. National Archives and Records Administration

Leafing Through
a review of books, blogs, magazines, film, etc.

Rebecca Rupp's collection of tales in *How Carrots Won the Trojan War* delivers an entertaining and authoritative history on mankind's relationship to garden edibles from asparagus to zucchini. The book covers the science and history of nutrition—the roles of war, globalization and political influence on vegetables and grains—and it delves into the more romantic side of food through culture, folklore and fairy tales.

How Carrots Won the Trojan War: Curious (but True) Stories of Common Vegetables
by Rebecca Rupp
(Storey Publishing, 2011)

As Rupp takes us on a flavorful journey through Rapunzel's fairy tale (which begins with a pregnant woman's craving for radishes) we find new meaning both in the lore and the radish. We learn about the beginning of farming when reading, "Lentils, along with barley and einkorn wheat, were among the first plants domesticated some 10,000 years ago in western Asia's lush Fertile Crescent," and we are introduced to historical figures such as the ancient Greek Pythagoras, the "Father of Vegetarianism," Leo Tolstoy (also a vegetarian), and Mark Twain, who famously said that broccoli is "nothing but a cabbage with a college education." We are amused to learn that Johann Sebastian Bach's famous Goldberg Variations was based on an old folk song, "Kraut and Ruben."

Rupp's sense of humor brings us laugh-out-loud quotes such as this one from Laurie Coleman, in *More Home Cooking* (1995), "They (lima beans) are pillowy, velvety, and delicious, and people should stop saying mean things about them." Rupp's stories make vegetables seem more like people as we investigate their struggles and heritage; carrots are glorified (did you know there is a world Carrot Museum?) and George Washington's favorite, asparagus (or sparrowgrass), is immortalized.

But there's more in this jam-packed, 349-page book. Culinary culture is explored through ancient recipes; we see what a dinner party was like in 1663 and learn that Thomas Jefferson's fondness for dining on vegetables was very much against the norm in early America. In the science department, we learn how spinach got a bad rap by a misplaced decimal point, that L-dopa was discovered through the fava bean, and that the fabulous watermelon has 40 percent more lycopene than tomatoes (or "love apples"). Facts like "Scotchgard was born from cabbage" and "sour kraut was used to fight scurvy," keep you turning pages.

If you are looking for inspiration to plant a garden, you will find it here. It's also a perfect pocket-book; flip it open at any page to find an interesting read. It would make a perfect gift for any gardener or vegetable lover.

—*Kathleen Lindemann*

Eaarth: Making a Life on a Tough New Planet
by Bill McKibben
(Times Books, 2010)

In 1989 McKibben published *The End of Nature*, regarded as the first book about climate change written for a general audience. At that time, even with all the empirical evidence supporting climate change, it appeared that with proper action, the unsavory effects resulting from a warming planet could be avoided and that climate change might be reversed. Now, just a little over two decades later, faced with the reality that the global average temperature has risen about 1°C and climate change's effects are now commonplace and well-documented, McKibben's message has changed. We no longer live on the same planet anymore, and our only alternative at this point is to get used to it.

Eaarth (with two a's) is the moniker that McKibben gives our new planet. Certainly we can call it whatever we want, but we must come to grips with the fact that this is not the same planet that it once was. The tundra is thawing, glaciers are disappearing, deserts and tropical zones are expanding, oceans are acidifying, warming, and rising, weather patterns are becoming more unpredictable, and drinking water is becoming salinated and depleted. "Global warming is no longer a philosophical threat, no longer a future threat, no longer a threat at all. It's our reality," and it's largely because "we didn't take our foot off the gas when we had the chance."

McKibben shares this news soberly and yet as light-heartedly as possible. Like anyone else who studies the effects of climate change, he'd rather be wrong, but the evidence is stacked against us. We are now faced with a grave set of options: choose now to readjust our societies to fit our new reality, or continue on as we have been and watch as our new reality makes the readjustment for us. McKibben makes the case in *Eaarth: Making Life on a Tough New Planet* that backing off is the better option, that a growth-based economy is no longer plausible, that ambitious, centralized, national and global projects are moot at this point. According to McKibben our best chance for survival is to go local, get small, and stay connected.

While the first half of *Eaarth* is spent laying out the trouble we're in—making certain that we comprehend the gravity of our situation, the second half is meant to offer us hope, something to cling to as we stumble toward the precipice. The challenge is to make these arguments convincingly. From my perspective, McKibben does so famously; however, with all the uncertainty inherent in our predicament and the fact that Eaarth is inhabited by seven billion individuals, all members of various societies and cultures, distinct and diverse in their myriad approaches and objectives, outlining a single good way to address our problems and getting everyone on board is beyond improbable. This is something that anyone endeavoring to tell people how to live must first understand. There is no silver bullet.

With that said, anyone entrenched in the current environmental movement, will find McKibben's suggestions familiar and obvious. Smaller farms and local, organic food production. Considerable reductions in energy consumption and decentralized, renewable production of energy. Local economies/communities and mindful consumption of material goods. The one item that might be a bit surprising is McKibben's love-affair with the Internet, but considering all the potential that the world wide web has for spreading information, providing entertainment, and fending off prejudice while cultivating tolerance, doing whatever we can to keep the Internet around seems like a pretty swell idea.

Eaarth is not meant to be yet another doom-and-gloom book. True, it does address our doom, and it will make you feel gloomy, but that's unavoidable with a topic like this. For someone like McKibben, who has made it his mission in life to educate the global populace about the painful truths and harsh realities of climate change, doing so must be thankless and heart-breaking considering how few will listen and how little will be done about it. And yet, somehow McKibben has kept his spirits up and has produced an incredibly readable, engrossing, and compelling book that has the potential to inspire its readers to move more "lightly, carefully, gracefully" on our formidable new planet.
—*Dan Murphy*

[Editor's Note: In this issue we're reviewing two books by Ben Hewitt—there was no intention to give special treatment to this author (or Rodale), it was simply a matter of the reviewers' choices.]

The Town That Food Saved: How One Community Found Vitality in Local Food
by Ben Hewitt
(Rodale Press, 2010)

Many books have been written about individual quests to eat locally (Barbara Kingsolver's *Animal, Vegetable, Miracle: A Year of Food Life* and Alisa Smith's *The 100 Mile Diet: A Year of Local Eating* easily come to mind). Ben Hewitt takes a different approach with *The Town that Food Saved* by chronicling the efforts in a small northwestern Vermont town (population around 3,200) to establish a local food system that will not only feeds its residents, but also create jobs, build community, and transform the economy. Such a system also reduces the demand on energy resources and reduces costs associated with the transportation and preservation of food.

Hewitt is a small-scale farmer with a conversational style—as if he is taking a stroll with the reader through the town of Hardwick and its verdant surrounding farmland. Like any community, Hardwick is rich in history, characters and rumors—and Hewitt presents each with compassion and humor. He shares a range of experiences from butchering pigs to visiting a cheese cave, from inhaling compost to volunteering in the local co-op, all while skillfully examining the pros and cons of a local food system.

In 2008, the town of Hardwick captured the attention of national media for its emergence as a successful agricultural model, thanks in large part to the promotional efforts of Tom Stearns, the de facto spokesman and owner of High Mowing Organic Seeds. Stearns is among a handful of what Hewitt terms an agripreneur "(a word… coined to describe the agrarian entrepreneurialism that infuses many of the region's food-based enterprises)." Although creating a decentralized food system based on businesses producing cheese, yogurt, soy, honey, composting and organic seeds (to name a few) may be a bright and hopeful concept, Hewitt also deftly describes some of the pitfalls.

As adamant as Stearns and others are about the benefits of Hardwick as a local food model, some locals are less than enthusiastic. Hewitt's neighbor Suzanna Jones (also a small scale farmer) is unimpressed with Stearns and his plans. She says, "Tom Stearns's approach to agriculture has so many elements of that (currency) system that it's not an alternative … What do people really need? They don't need convenience; they need food, clothing, shelter. They don't need this gentrified green, boutique scene." Jones's attitude is not opposed to the idea of a local food system; she believes that Hardwick has a long-established system already—it is the home of the Buffalo Mountain Food Co-op, one of the oldest operating food cooperatives in the county. Instead, she sees communities such as Newark, N.J., in greater need of such a system because it is so reliant on other entities.

Hewitt's willingness to show both sides of the story is one of the great strengths of this book. Another is his ability to describe the landscape, the people, their passion for locally grown food, and the possibilities a different type of food system holds. If you care about exploring these possibilities, read this book.

—*Robin Intemann*

Making Supper Safe: One Man's Quest To Learn The Truth About Food Safety
by Ben Hewitt
(Rodale, 2011)

As I write this review, one of the deadliest food-borne illness outbreaks in the last ten years, listeria, has claimed the lives of 25 people across the United States, and over a hundred more are ill. The deadly bacteria was traced to a crop of cantaloupe from a farm in Colorado. There's a lot that's unsettling about this particular food-illness outbreak; the number of deaths, the people still suffering, and how widely and how quickly it spread.

In *Making Supper Safe*, Ben Hewitt sets out to inform Americans of our increasingly vulnerable food industry, vulnerable due to the "consolidation of agribusiness and the ever expanding distance between people and their sources of nourishment…"

Hewitt begins and ends the book with a strong visual as he tags along with a dumpster-diver in Vermont. After all, what sounds more dangerous than eating out of a dumpster? But what I really think Hewitt illustrates with these bookend chapters is awareness. Interestingly, the dumpster-diver or "freegan" is very conscious of food safety and risk and not as vulnerable as Hewitt believes the average American is.

Pathogenic bacteria are everywhere, and while many may be familiar with the bacterium E. coli, Hewitt explains that salmonella and listeria actually kill far more Americans each year. In simple language without a lot of scientific jargon, Hewitt explains why and how outbreaks happen and who is to blame.

Hewitt also addresses the raw milk debate, raw food, food rights, antibiotic use in food-producing animals, high fructose corn syrup, the increase in multinational food processors, and the global seed industry concentration. Each of these topics could be a book-length subject in itself, but Hewitt does a good job introducing the topics and explaining how each adds to the debate.

Hewitt doesn't draw conclusions on food safety; he only presents information in an easy-to-read journalistic style. He clearly has his opinions, revealed in statements like, "…the most palpable threat in [Americans] food is the policy behind it, a policy that has given rise to a system of constant abundance that, even as it fills our stomachs to bursting, offering a false promise of wellness and short-term satisfaction, starves us of our long-term health."

For readers already conscious of where their food comes from, this book confirms what they already believed. But Hewitt also presents an argument for eating local and offers new information on "food corporatism" that I found surprising, including the fact that there are four times as many prisoners in the United States as farmers. Overall I found this book an interesting overview of the American food industry and our inherent risks as consumers—one that will most certainly prompt more research and discussion.
—*Pat Kennelly*

The Heirloom Life Gardener
by Jere and Emilee Gettle.
(Hyperion, 2011)

In *The Heirloom Life Gardener* Jere Gettle, the owner and founder of the highly celebrated heirloom seed company Baker Creek Seeds, takes you on a journey from his boyhood passion of saving seeds to immersion in heirloom vegetables and the preservation and dispersal of these seeds as an adult. Steeped in historical references and facts, this book helps readers begin to appreciate the importance of preserving our heritage plants.

Being a life-long gardener myself, I was wondering what this book had to offer. I am thoroughly delighted to say that this easy read was both inspirational and timely. We have been at a crossroads for quite some time. Will we join the challenge of preserving and perpetuating heirloom plants or just let them perish? If Jere and Emilee have anything to say about it we are in good hands.

They make the gardening world easily accessible to all through commonsense suggestions and tips. The specific seed-saving techniques in the last chapter: "A to Z Growing Guide" is the crowning touch. A diverse garden of Gettle's favorite heirloom vegetables varieties are described, along with their cultivation requirements, cooking suggestions, and of course, their requirements in saving seed.

This book will definitely find a prominent spot in my garden library.
—*Larry Stebbins*

Growthbusters:
Hooked on Growth
Directed by Dave Gardner
(Citizen-Powered Media, 2011)

We've lived with it all our lives: The Holy Religion of Growth. Growth is Good. No Growth = Death. We want to grow our cities, our businesses, our lives (this being closely related to a twin affliction, Bigger is Better, relating to bigger cars, houses, TVs, breasts, etc.)

It's understandable that the mythology has a firm grip on our psyche. Prosperity and growth have existed simultaneously for so long they've become (falsely) fused. And this idea actually worked fine when the planet was "empty." Now that we're "full" and getting more depleted by the hour it's a different story. We're finally seeing the light: Infinite growth in a finite space is just not possible. Furthermore, growth is now a negative force on our prosperity—loss of resources, species extinction, climate change and overpopulation are serious financial drains.

Through leading thinkers (scientists, sociologists, economists) and a winning sense of humor, Dave Gardner's film *Growthbusters* (a play on *Ghostbusters*) separates fact from superstitition in a highly palatable way. It explores how our cultural beliefs are the true culprits, and reveals just who perpetuates the "Growth is God" mythology (hint—those who can afford to purchase their own self-serving brand of "truth").

GrowthBusters finally asks the most critical question of our time: How do we become a sustainable civilization? The answer is recognizing that our current levels of consumption and population growth are the problem, and taking control.

Just as we see in McKibben's book *Eaarth,* while things seem tough, it's also a time for opportunity; an opportunity to jump off the consumer hamster wheel and claim more self-sufficiency, more time for our friends and family, and a greater connection to our communities—the truest trappings of prosperity.
—*Sandra Knauf*

Top Dressing

The Lesson of a Peach by Eva Syrovy

"Ms. S.," asked the sweet sixth-grader who had unaccountably earned lunch detention in my classroom, "can you eat the skin?"

"What?" I was deep in the midst of readying for my four afternoon classes.

She held up a beautiful, whole peach. "Is it OK to eat the skin?"

"Yes, of course. Haven't you ever had a fresh peach before?"

"No." Then she bit into it.

She had my attention now. "How is it?"

"Good! Sweet and a little sour . . . mm, it's really juicy!"

Watching her munch on the perfectly ripe fruit, my thoughts were catapulted to a couple of weeks before. I'd been tasked with attending the local Farms-to-Schools meeting. It was at the end of a long day, the kids in my last period class had misbehaved, I couldn't find a parking space, and I'd arrived late, disgusted and impatient with the liberal claptrap I was sure I'd hear.

There was a college professor who encouraged all school district employees to fight for our principles, to make waves. As I listened, I thought, "She has no idea of the hierarchical nature of teaching, that making waves is hardly ever a good idea in the era of shrinking budgets and high credit card bills."

Then Rick Hughes, the food and nutrition director for my school district, told of his trip to Palisade. He'd found an organic orchard and purchased peaches for the lunches of all the students in our school district as part of the district's Good Food Project.

He relished telling the tale of the orchard owner who'd been out picking fruit when he called her. "I'll serve the peaches whole—just like that—for dessert!" he enthused.

At the time, I had listened a little dyspeptically and wished not for a peach but for a cup of something caffeinated.

I left as soon as I could, not looking forward to the next meeting.

Now, I watched the girl finish the fruit and realized that it wasn't really surprising that it was the first time she'd eaten a fresh peach.

I recalled that, last summer, I'd walked by and looked longingly at the grocery-store display of Honeycrisp apples. Since each apple weighed about a pound, they cost about $3 per serving—and that was a little rich for my budget.

Around the corner stood a display of peanut butter and chocolate bars, the kind I love and used to indulge in fairly frequently, before I lost 60 pounds by basically eschewing all processed foods. The bars, each of which was two- to three-times the calories of one of the apples, cost $3—for a case of 12.

If I were a financially stressed parent trying to feed a family, I had to consider, which would I choose? The apples or the sugar- and fat-filled snack bars?

All I can say to Mr. Hughes now is, "Kudos!"

The only downside? There weren't quite enough peaches. When I asked Jake, my own seventh-grader, whether he'd tasted any of the delicious fruit, he said, "I saw them. But by the time I got to the front of the lunch line, they were gone."

That broke my heart. But then again, Jake gets plenty of fruit at home. ✽